MW01132694

THE CARDHOLDER

By Kelly O'Callan

KELLY O'CALLAN

The characters and events in this book are fictitious. Any similarity to real persons, living or dead, is coincidental and not intended by the author.

The Cardholder
Copyright 2013 by Kelly O'Callan
CreateSpace Edition

ISBN-13 : 978-1493521739
ISBN-10 :149352173x

DEDICATION

I would like to dedicate this book to my parents, Kathleen and Nicholas Russo. You may not have been able to deal me the best cards in life, but you certainly taught me how to play my hand well.

Thank you.

Dear Tina,
Hope you
enjoy the read!

Kelly O'Callan

ACKNOWLEDGEMENTS

I would like to give much thanks to my editor, Nina Meditz, for her never-ending support and the hard work she invested in this book. And, an additional thanks to Melissa Meditz, for her helpful contribution to the cover design. To my children, Mason and Liam, thank you for sharing this journey with me. I love you.

KELLY O'CALLAN

"In good years the children of the people are most of them good, and in the bad years they are most of them evil. It is not owing to their natural endowments conferred by Heaven, that they are thus different. It is owing to the circumstances in which they allow their mind to be ensnared and devoured that they appear so (as in the latter case)."

Mencius (372-289 BCE) Book 6

KELLY O'CALLAN

PROLOGUE

I hate cigarette smoke. The fumes get me hotter than the flame that births the poison. I hope I don't offend any of you that do smoke, but I have my reasons why I do not possess a tolerance for it.

Maybe it's just the fact that right now I'm sitting in a room filled with the air polluting white stuff. Or maybe it's because the strange bitch next to me, who just dropped some sexual innuendos in my ear, is puffing away. Or maybe, it's just because I'm in this damn place right now.

A year ago, I would have never dreamed that I would be sitting here at this moment. It's amazing how the entire course of your life can change just from meeting one person...

KELLY O'CALLAN

CHAPTER ONE

It was the summer of 1999. Stick-straight hair was hip. Blue nail polish was all the rage. It was the summer we lost our beloved John-John. It was the summer when computer geeks and wizards frantically searched for a solution to the impending arrival of the millennium bug. It was also the summer the U.S. Northeast had the worst drought in documented history.

I was living comfortably in a town called Ardmore, an upscale suburb located just outside of Philadelphia, with my husband of fourteen years, Greg, and our twelve-year-old son, Derek. At the age of thirty-six, I felt as though I was just entering the prime of my life. I had a happy and healthy marriage to my high-school sweetheart, a wonderful son old enough to be left unsupervised at home, and a thriving counseling practice I'd spent years building.

I was looking forward to the fourth-annual block party that was held on Birch Street, where I resided, and was hoping that the excessive heat would not disrupt any of the planned activities. Unfortunately, the high temperature and humidity level on that last Saturday in July was enough to fry the brains inside our sweltering heads. Still, the partying carried on. Derek was off doing cannonballs in a neighbor's pool, Greg was aggressively whacking a volleyball on the block's winning team - between tending to chicken and burgers on the grill - and I was simply relaxing on the hammock in my front yard. Sipping thirstily on a home-brewed iced tea, I was grateful for the peaceful moment I was enjoying, until I heard a familiar squeaky voice.

"Hey over there, Maggie Simmons! Congratulations! I see you won the 'Best of Philly' award for Best Couples Therapist in Philadelphia Magazine!"

It was the voice of Jill Coopersmith, our neighborhood gnat. Every street has one. You know, that woman on your street who knows everything about everybody within a five-block radius. The neighborhood gnat peers through her curtains at you when you come home at 3 a.m. and thinks she can dictate who should park where. She doesn't miss a trick, that gnat. Always within eye's view of your driveway or front door, conveniently waiting to grab you on your way in or out, desperately needing a fix of details on you or to dish the dirt about other innocent neighbors. Always crap you couldn't give a damn about, unless you were a gnat yourself.

"Thanks, Jill," I smiled modestly. "I never saw that one coming."

Jill's close-set, apple green eyes narrowed as her voice shrieked. "Oh please, you can't expect me to believe that one. Every couple that I've spoken to, that are clients of yours, swear to me that you're the best! And let me tell you, I know many a couple who goes to therapy. Half of the marriages on this street alone aren't what they're cracked up to be..."

I could feel it coming. Jill was going to give me a run down on names and try to pull opinions out of me, but I wasn't going to fall for it. I began searching for a scapegoat to save me from her scuttlebutt, but couldn't find one at that particular moment. I'd just have to suffer in the meantime.

"Rick and Marcy may be splitting up," she rambled, "The Morgans are arguing because David wants to relocate to Florida and Anita wants to stay put. Ralph's been running around on poor Nancy. Is anybody happy anymore?"

Jill's voice paused in thought as I unwillingly listened to the demise of my neighbors' relationships. Suddenly, her pink-skinned face was covered in merriment. "Ya know what I think, Maggie? I think we should all be like that Alexis LeNoir. Now, she's one smart cookie."

Alexis LeNoir, an attractive, blonde aristocrat in her late forties, owned the most valuable property on Birch Street. Her brownstone mansion sat atop the curved hill, delivering an eccentric flair to the neighborhood's ensemble of modern Tudors, Queen Annes, and Dutch Colonials. I didn't know much about the woman except that she was an

12

only child who inherited her French father's old monetary estate. She never married or bore any children. I'd heard wild rumors of her having many lovers - all of which I'm sure came from Jill.

Jill squinted her eyes and puckered her lips as though she just sucked from a fresh lemon. "Mmm...mmm. Have you had a look at that new stud she's been hiding under her roof?"

I cackled at Jill's behavior. "What are you talking about?"

She grabbed my arm, coaxing me to stand away from my hammock and we shifted our bodies towards the volleyball game at the end of the street. She placed a stiffened hand above her brow to shield the sun's glare and pointed excitedly with the other.

"He's the cutie-pie, two guys to left of your husband. You can't miss him."

I also placed a hand along my brows to block the blinding sun from interfering with my visual calculation. My eyes quickly darted through the small gathering in the middle of the street and I instantly caught glimpse of my husband. Standing broad at 6'2", Greg was easy to spot in a crowd.

Jill nudged me. "So, do you see him?"

Just then, my eyes took me to a man who stood just a few feet from Greg. He was about 5'10" with a somewhat lanky frame, accentuated by perfect posture. He wore loose-fitting beige Dockers and a form-fitting white tee-shirt that magnified the richness of his tanned skin. His hips were narrow and his shoulders were broadened by bulging sculpted muscles that were quite noticeable through his tee. His hair appeared to be thick and wavy and I couldn't quite make out his face from where I stood.

"Doesn't he look delicious?" Jill asked.

"Sure," I said, not sure of myself.

"Mmmmmm," she sighed. "I can't say he's the best-looking guy I've ever laid eyes on, but he sure seems yummy. There's just something about him. I ran into him last week at Carlino's Market and close-up, he sort of reminds me of James Dean. I guess it's that bad boy, mysterious thing."

13

I felt a sudden, forceful poke at the side of my ribs. I turned to find my son, Derek, red-eyed from chlorine, standing with a scowl on his face.

"Mom, where's my Gameboy? I can't find it anywhere and I want to show it to Pete. I know you probably took it and hid it from me."

I was grateful for my son's intrusion. "I'm not sure where it is, but I'll go inside with you and help you find it."

I apologized to Jill for my abrupt departure, but was secretly relieved that I'd been excused from the entrapment of the chatty gnat.

Later that evening, my sister, Annie, dropped by unannounced. Annie often did that after a date when she needed some tried and true sympathy that she just couldn't capture from a simple phone call. Sometimes, she would pop over after midnight, which drove my husband batty. I hate to admit it, but her late night arrivals had even bothered me occasionally, especially when Derek was younger.

"Oh, Maggie, you won't believe the night I just had," Annie moaned, as she slipped through the front door dressed in a pink-laced top and a skirt so short her legs looked endless. It was just after ten and I was dressed for bed and cuddled up on the couch with a good book.

"Annie, what a surprise it is to see you here," Greg spoke, his voice soaked in sarcasm, while peering up from his newspaper.

I shot him the keep-quiet-wise-ass glance. Annie flipped him the bird and gave a curt smile.

I closed my book and put it down beside me, figuring I wouldn't be reading another word that evening. "What happened, honey?"

Annie plopped down on the couch next to me with a familiar look of disappointment on her face. "Mags, I just had one of the best dates I've had in years and something totally shitty happened."

"As usual," Greg murmured behind his paper.

I placed my hand on her bare thigh. "What happened, Sweetie?"

"Well, Scott took me to Cafe Dellatori's for dinner. You know, that

14

great chic restaurant on Chestnut Street with the exquisite Mediterranean cuisine. Anyway, everything is going well. He's handsome, witty, successful, romantic, and we were having the best evening possible. And then..."

"Here comes the clincher," mumbled Greg.

I threw a pillow at him. "Go on, Annie."

"And then this crazy woman comes trotting over to our table and starts yelling all this crap at Scott. Then she turns to me and tells me that she's Scott's fiancee!"

Greg dropped his newspaper. "Wow. Sounds like this is gonna get good."

Annie continued. "Then she takes off her diamond ring and flings it at him and tells him never to call her again!"

Greg let out a slight chuckle.

"Do you mind over there?" Annie snapped as she smeared the crimson off her lips with a crumpled tissue. "Do you really think this is funny?"

Greg smiled, with the innocence of a child. "What? Don't you think it's a bit funny yourself?"

Neither of us answered him.

"Look," Greg said, getting the hint and rising to his feet, "it's late and it's been a long day. I'm just gonna mosey off to bed and let you ladies finish your chatting. Good night."

He kissed Annie on the cheek, gave me the let's-have-sex-tonight wink, and went off to bed.

Feeling rather horny myself, I was anxious for Annie to finish up her story and hit the road. It had been weeks since Greg was in the mood so I needed to take advantage of his carnal invitation. "So what else happened? What did you say to him?"

"I was pretty shocked. At first, I thought it was all an act. Like something that could only happen in a movie. I just couldn't believe it was real. So, I asked him if what the woman said was true. And he said yes, it was true. My heart just sank."

Poor Annie. She had the worst luck with men. Anyone who knew

Annie could not understand her difficulty in cultivating a decent relationship. Annie was twenty-nine years old, a svelte, leggy blonde with drop-dead gorgeous looks, and a vivacious personality that just sucked you in. You could not help but fall in love with her. Women wanted to be like her and men wanted to be in her. Any man that crossed her path became captivated by her beauty and it seemed as though Annie could virtually own whoever she damn well pleased. That was rarely the case, however.

"So, what else happened?" I inquired.

"Well, I asked him why he asked me out if he was already engaged to someone else. And do you know what he said? You're not gonna believe this one..."

Annie sank back into the couch, crossed her long, lean legs and pushed a golden curl back from her forehead. She spoke coolly. "He told me that he wanted to make sure that the other woman was totally right for him and thought he should try one more fling for reassurance. And he said I was too hot of a babe to pass up an opportunity on. Can you believe that jerk?!?"

Unfortunately, I could. Annie, on the other hand, did not have a true grasp of what men were really like - yet. If she knew it or not, she was still living under 'the prince charming' delusion, and thinking this impeccable man without flaws would pop into her life, sweep her off her feet, and they would live happily ever after. It's not that she wasn't enjoying all the Mr. Wrongs in the meantime; she had a black book that would make Madonna blush. I think at this point, she was feeling the pressure of turning thirty soon, and feared that she may never meet Mr. Right while she was wrinkle-free and of child-bearing age. Much of this pressure came from her married friends, and our dear old mom.

"I don't get it," she pouted. "I don't know if I'll ever meet the right guy. What's wrong with me?"

"Sure you will," I encouraged her. "Don't be so hard on yourself. Nothing's wrong with you. The right guy will come along one day."

"Ha! That's easy for you to say," she retorted. "You married your high-school sweetheart right out of college. You were a mom by the time you were twenty-five, and you had your own psychiatric practice by the time you were thirty! You have the perfect life!"

"I really don't understand what your problem is, Annie," I countered. "You have an awesome life! You can come and go as you please, having no one to answer to and no one else to be responsible for. You look like a goddamn Barbie doll with men dropping at your feet, wining and dining you. And then you can screw anyone you want without having to worry about cooking, cleaning, and doing their laundry for them..."

I was pummeling away with my words when Annie suddenly fastened her French manicured hand over my mouth in an effort to cease my bickering. She began to laugh.

"You know what, Mags? You're right. I do have a pretty awesome life. And besides, if I wasn't around, who else would you be able to live vicariously through?"

My eyes narrowed and I pointed to the door. "Get out. Get out of my house right now, you little hussy."

Annie put her arms around me and pulled me towards her, planting a kiss on my cheek. "I love you, Mags. I don't know what I'd do without you. You always make me feel better."

"Yeah, well, I guess that's what big sisters are for," I said with a crooked smile.

"Oh! Before I go," Annie said rising to her feet. "Don't forget we have Trista's bridal shower to go to next Sunday."

I growled. "I hate those damn things. Why do I have to go to Trista's bridal shower? She's your friend."

"Because she likes you! And, because Mom is going too, and you know Mom. She'll want you there if she's going."

"But this weekend Greg and I are celebrating our fourteenth wedding anniversary. I don't want to spend part of it at a shower. Or with Mom!"

Annie flashed a puckish grin as she headed out the door. "Pick you up around noontime!"

CHAPTER TWO

The next morning started out as typical as all the recent Mondays I've had- Greg quickly slurping down his two or three cups of coffee while frantically trying to get out the door to reach his job as a stockbroker at J.T. Morgan (where he had recently been promoted to managerial status), while I dealt with the daily dilemma of deciding what to wear to work. I ended up choosing a simple, navy blue dress that fit me a little more snugly than it should have. It was given to me by Annie, who typically wore a size four or six, and I usually fit comfortably into a size six or eight. I gave myself one final look in the mirror, as I brushed my shoulder length chestnut hair, and decided I looked fine. I popped my head into Derek's room shouting out the routine warning that he and his friends better not wreck the house while I was gone. He sleepily mumbled his usual "I won't!" and I headed off to work.

The drive to work took roughly thirty minutes depending on traffic. Even though I only lived nine or ten miles from my office, the congestion on the Schyukill Expressway was enough to make the most patient driver cringe with angst. I was downtown on 8th Street in Center City and handled half the practice of the McClain Psychological Center. The business was started by Donald McClain back in the early eighties and, after many years of successful growth, Don sought out another psychologist to help him with the overflow. He hired me to work part-time in 1991, when Derek started pre-school, at which time I was finally in a position to get my career started and end my stint as a stay-at-home-mom. When Derek was old enough to attend grade-school, I changed my hours to full-time and settled on the specialty of being a marriage/couples' therapist. The complexity of the relationship between a man and woman always fascinated me, and I enjoyed the challenge of smoothing out the intricacies.

THE CARDHOLDER

For the past six months or so, my first standing appointment of the week belonged to Sue Adelsberg. She arrived promptly at 9 a.m. with her frizzy, orange-sherbet colored hair slackened by hairpins, and the typical distraught intensity that blazed within her anxiety-ridden, blue eyes. She was waiting for me inside my office when I arrived, and I flashed a knowing grin at Sandy, our receptionist, before entering the room.

"Good morning, Sue! How are you this morning?"

"Okay, I guess, Dr. Simmons."

"And how were things with Harry this week? Any improvement? Or anything you wanted to tell me about?"

Sue let out a long sigh. I knew that long sigh. I'd heard that sigh on many occasions, so I mentally prepared myself for the saga that was about to spill from her narrow, pink mouth.

"Nothing's any better with us this week. I wanted to try some of the techniques you told me about, but Harry showed no interest in cooperating with me!"

Sue Adelsberg was clearly a hagridden woman, sorely afflicted with self-made chaos. At age thirty-six, she married a man fourteen years her senior, hoping to acquire that American dream she had spent her whole life searching for. She wanted a doting husband complete with two beautiful children, one boy and one girl, of course. After two years of marriage, the realization of the fact that she wedded an old hat, who just wanted a woman to care for him, frenzied her.

"I can't get him to do anything with me," she rambled on with her thin, whiny voice, "All he wants to do is just lie around and read or watch the television all day. We haven't had sex in over a month! I could parade around naked in front of the t.v. and all he would do is tell me to move because I'm blocking the screen."

"Have you tried my suggestion with the deck of foreplay cards?"

"Yes, and all he said was that the only deck he was interested in playing with were Pinochle cards," she whimpered.

"Sue, perhaps you should have Harry come back in for a session with you during your next visit," I suggested.

"Well, frankly, Harry doesn't like you doctors. He thinks you are bad. He says that you mind-doctors make everything worse in a relationship because you... what were his exact words... ah, yes, that you psychoanalyze the shit out of everything and that screws peoples' heads up even more."

I was stumped, and Sue sensed it.

"But don't worry, Dr. Simmons," she reassured me. "I don't think that way at all about you. I would be lost without you! Who else could keep me sane enough from wanting to blow my husband's head off?"

After my session with Sue, I walked her to the front desk, again encouraging her to bring Harry with her the following week.

"Okay, I'll try to convince him," she squeaked as she headed towards the exit. "I'll go out and buy some tranquilizers and slip them in his morning coffee. He'll probably never know."

After she left the building, I walked behind Sandy's chair and placed my hands over her ears before I let out a long groan.

Sandy giggled. "I don't know how you and Don handle some of those people every week, Maggie. Some of them have too many screws loose."

"Yeah, well, my job is to be the screwdriver and put those loose screws back into place. And I'm a damn good screwdriver," I replied. "So, who is my next scheduled screwball?"

"Mickey Dillon."

"Who? Is he new?"

"He is a new client. He called first thing when I walked in this morning and said he wanted an appointment right away. He specifically asked for you. I told him you had a ten-thirty open this morning and he took it."

"Hmmm, a new client that said he needed to come in and see me right away," I wondered while giving Sandy a furtive look. "Maybe his fiancee left him standing at the altar over the weekend and he wants to know what went wrong."

Sandy's eyes beamed with eagerness. "And if that's it, are you gonna give me the scoop, Maggie?"

"Sorry, Sandy, you know I can't tell you a thing that goes on within the four walls of my room. But, you can always eavesdrop without my knowing it," I joked.

"Now why would I do a thing like that?" she winked in response.

I headed back inside my office. "Please send Mr. Dillon inside when he arrives. I'll be waiting for him."

Little did I know of how my life would drastically change after that meeting.

CHAPTER THREE

Rare are the moments in life, when you meet someone or pass them on the street, that you sense a sudden rush of familiarity with such a strong intensity that you felt that the moment was actually surreal. I experienced that same uncanny rush the moment Mickey Dillon stepped into my office. When our eyes locked, it seemed as though time stood still, and I was fed an unearthly meal of fate and purpose - as if our crossing paths in life was undeniably meant to be.

I felt as if I fell into a trance as his golden green eyes seduced mine. I tried to shake it off as I rose from my seat and extended my hand over my desk towards him. "Good morning, you must be Mr. Dillon. I'm Dr. Margaret Simmons, nice to meet you."

He cocked a half-smile out of nervousness and greeted me back. I directed him to the seat in front of me. "So, Mr. Dillon, may I ask what brought you here to see me this morning?"

"Well, Dr. Simmons, I have a little problem that I need help with and I was told that you were the best person to go to."

His voice was smooth and deep, yet gentle.

"Oh, so I was a recommended to you. May I ask who sent you here?"

He paused for a moment. "To be honest with you, I don't really remember her name. But she lives on our street. She told me you won the 'Best of Philly' award for Best Couples Therapist."

"Jill Coopersmith?"

"Yeah, I think that's what her name was. Jill."

I was awestruck. "How do you know... wait a minute. Did you say that you lived on *our* street? I thought you looked a little familiar to me."

He looked a bit uneasy. "I do?"

"Yes. You're that fellow who's living with that woman in the brownstone mansion on top of the hill, Alexis LeNoir, aren't you?"

"Yes. Have we met before?"

I chuckled. "No, but just the other day you were pointed out to me by a woman who knows a lot about Birch Street. Jill Coopersmith."

The enigmatic stranger let out a slight snicker. "I see."

"In any case, Mr. Dillon," I said, as I poised myself to get back to business, "may I ask again what has brought you here to seek my help? Are you and Alexis having problems in your relationship?"

"You can call me Mick," he replied, while averting his eyes around the room. On occasion, he would glance at me, and when he did, it was candidly. "I've come to seek your help with a problem I have. It really has nothing to do with Alex, just me. I want to learn how to fall in love."

There was an inept moment of silence between us.

"Okay, Mick," I responded. "So, am I correct in hearing that the reason you have chosen to come and see me today is because you want to learn how to fall in love?"

"Yes, Dr. Simmons, that's correct."

I thought for a moment. "Mr. Dillon, I am honored that you have chosen to seek counseling from me. However, the type of counsel you seek is not exactly my area of expertise. I deal strictly with the problem areas that a loving couple may encounter together and try to help them work through their differences. You, on the other hand, are seeking need of help in a more one-to-one personal matter. If you'd like, I could give you the name of a very good..."

"I don't want anyone else," Mick interrupted, leaning forward from his chair. "I want the best that's out there. The best is you."

"Thank you," I grinned, "But..."

"But what? I need to be part of a couple to seek advice from you? Quite honestly, Dr. Simmons, doesn't it make sense that I'm not here in the form of a couple with another person because I'm obviously having trouble getting to that stage? You are an expert on relationships between a man and a woman, am I correct?"

"Yes. And I also provide counsel for homosexual relationships as well."

"Well, then you are the doctor I want to see. You are going to be the person that helps me understand a woman and her needs. How can I possibly fall, and stay in love with woman when I can't understand one?"

"Mick, may I ask what exactly has sparked your interest in wanting to fall in love with someone?"

He relaxed back into his seat. "I turned thirty-two last week. For the past ten years or so, I've been living my life as a gigolo, shackin' up with any woman that would have me. I'm getting pretty tired of living that way."

Mick reached into his shirt pocket, pulling out a cigarette that he proceeded to light.

"I'm sorry, Mick, but this is a non-smoking building. There's a sign here on the wall." I pointed it out to him.

He looked at me with elusive eyes. "But, I was just gonna have a couple of drags. That's all."

"Sorry, those are the rules. If you'd like, you may step outside a few minutes and I can wait until you come back in to continue."

Mick took a long suck and smashed his freshly lit cigarette into the bottom of the small trash bin. "That's okay. I should really cut back on smoking. It's bad for me."

I continued. "So, Mick, have you ever fallen in love with any of the ladies you have shacked up with?"

Mick smiled in reminiscence as he slowly traced the seams of his pants with his fingertips. "Yes. I've practically fallen for every one of them."

"Interesting." I wondered. "It sounds to me like falling in love isn't really a problem for you."

"Well, maybe that's not totally true. Perhaps falling in lust is more like it. And I did actually love these women, in a caring way. But, true love... I do think that may have happened for me only once, and I blew it. I was so stupid."

"What happened? Was it a woman you once lived with?"

He tensed up a bit, sighing and pressing his face through his loose

24

palms. "No. It was a girl I met a long time ago, back when I was in college."

"You went to college?"

Mick laughed. His Cheshire cat grin was wide and lit up his whole face. "Yeah, can you believe a guy like me attended college? I never finished though. Not after I had my breakdown."

"You had a breakdown? What kind of breakdown?"

Mick paused as his laughing eyes suddenly turned grim. "A nervous breakdown. Man, I never want to go through that again. It was the worst time in my life and the girl... her name was Tracie... stuck by me the whole time and helped me get through it. She was a total saint and angel to me and I loved her with all my heart, but several months after getting better from my breakdown, I dumped her. I hurt her so badly, and I was wrong. But, I had to do it. Anytime I was with her, I felt like I was back at that bad point in my life. Like, when I saw her, I saw myself reliving that breakdown."

"That's understandable. But, of course, that doesn't mean it seems fair. May I ask you what caused your breakdown?"

I could see I was making the poor man ill with having to recollect a terrible experience, but he carried on. "Let's just say I got myself into some trouble. I have something that's called an addictive personality. Are you familiar with what that means?"

"Yes," I answered, recalling my days in psychology class. "That's when a person habitually becomes fixated on someone, or something. In essence, they become an addict to that particular someone or something."

Mick nodded. "Yes, and for me at that particular point in time, my addiction was with gambling. And I'm not talking a few bucks here or there. I'm talking thousands of dollars. It was nothing for me to take a midnight drive down to Atlantic City and drop a couple of thousand a night at a casino."

"And, where did you get that kind of money from?"

"It was mostly my father's money. I was stealing from him. I got so bad into debt from all my gambling, I was flunking school, and my dad was finding everything out which made him extremely pissed off. I thought he was going to kill me... and I just lost it. That's when I had my breakdown."

Mick ran his fingers across the top of his thickly gelled, golden-brown hair and was visibly shaken. "Man, I never want to go through that again. I'd rather have a gang of angry gorillas beat me repeatedly over the head with steel bats tenfold than to feel that way again."

His knees began to quake and his face became ashen from discomfort, as though a sickening wave of terror welled up from his belly. "Do you mind if I take that smoke break now?"

As Mick Dillon exited my office, I began contemplating whether or not to take him on as a new client. Although the specific reason he was seeking therapy was not my forte, in the few minutes he was in my company, I somehow became bedazzled by him. Why? I wasn't sure. But, decided that I would find out.

Always up for a challenge, I opted to take Mr. Dillon on as a client and help him in his quest to learn how to fall in love. If anything, it would be quite an experience for me, professionally and psychologically speaking. I hopped out from behind my desk and headed towards the back wall where my metal file cabinet stood. I gently bent over to pull out a blank folder from the drawer below.

"That's a pretty dress you have on."

Startled, I quickly lifted my head and swung my body around. "Huh? Excuse me?"

Mick smiled coyly, looking much more composed. "I like your dress. It's pretty. Blue is my favorite color."

I smiled back at him with reserve. "Thank you. It was a hand-me-down from my sister."

"Your sister has good taste," he replied as he retook his seat. I sat back in mine.

"So tell me, Mick, just how did you end up becoming a gigolo?"

He licked his lips. "Just after my breakdown, I figured the best way to get back on my feet was to make some cold, hard cash fast. A buddy I was staying with at the time offered me a job to tend bar at his nightclub, just outside of Chicago. One night, a group of good-looking women stopped in. I could tell they had big bucks and were looking for a good time. Within a short period of time, they were all apparently interested in taking me home for the evening. As a joke, I told the women that whoever would make the highest bid for me could take me home as a prize. I laughed, but the women didn't, and they took their bidding war seriously. As it turned out, the top girl bid a whopping eight-hundred bucks for me. I got to leave with her that night, go home with her to her beautiful, warm house, fuck like crazy in her beautiful, big bed, and leave there with an extra eight-hundred in my pocket. Only, I didn't exactly leave there for awhile. Over the course of the next several months, I practically lived with her, and occasionally did some sexual favors for her friends on the side for some extra cash. There is nothing more exciting to me than to please a woman, and I'll do anything it takes to bring a woman to climax."

He passed a searching stare my way and I could feel a chill run up my spine as my arms blossomed goose bumps.

"Anyhow, in return, these women spoiled me. I got whatever I wanted out of them."

"Such as?" I inquired.

"Anything. They gave me full use of their homes and their cars. They gave me money, jewelry, bought me nice clothes. I ate at the fanciest restaurants. You name it. If I wanted it, I got it. All I had to do was fuck them the way they wanted to be fucked, treat them the way they wanted to be treated, and all that came pretty easily to me."

I became intrigued. "Mick, were any of these women that you were, um, servicing, if that is the correct phrase... were any of them married?"

"Yes," he grinned almost proudly. "As a matter of fact, a couple of them were. Funny, sometimes the married ones were hungrier for attention and affection than the single girls."

He lightly ran his fingers along his broad jaw, settling his middle and forefinger into the soft cleft of his chin. He then glanced at a recent photo of my family sitting on my desk. "You're married, aren't you Dr. Simmons?"

"Yes. Fourteen years this weekend."

"Happily married?"

"Yes," I smiled guardedly. "But, we're not here to speak of my marriage, Mr. Dillon, but rather to speak of your dilemma."

He seemed embarrassed. "Oh, I apologize for my intrusion, Dr. Simmons. I meant no harm by it. I'm happy for you."

I was also a bit red-faced. "That's okay. I apologize myself. Sometimes I can be a bit apprehensive when it comes to discussing my personal business with a patient and I can get pretty defensive on that matter. I know it sounds like a double standard sort of thing."

"Did I just hear you refer to me as a patient? Does this mean that you're interested in helping me?"

"Yes," I nodded congenially. "I would be willing to take you on as a patient, Mr. Dillon."

Later that day, I met my sister, Annie, for our weekly Monday evening class at Paula's Yoga Studio. It was located in Bryn Mawr, a halfway point between my home in Ardmore and Annie's apartment in Conshohocken. Although it was a brief ten minute ride for each of us, Annie typically arrived for our 7 p.m. class a few minutes late. That was the case on that evening as well.

Our instructor, Paula, was a rubber-limbed woman in her forties with dark, striking features. She had thick, shiny black hair that she kept neatly tucked in a bun or slicked back in a ponytail, and big dark ebony eyes adorned with perfectly arched eyebrows that would wrinkle in vexation when Annie popped tardily into her room.

"I'm so sorry," Annie would squeak in a whisper and tiptoe her way to my side. She plopped to the right of me as I was breathing my way through the middle of my warming exercises.

"Hey, what's going on?" Annie whispered, quickly mimicking my corpse pose.

"Nothing much. How 'bout you? Why were you late this time?"

"Work."

"Overtime?"

"No, I got stuck talking to Charles in the break room. He just broke up with his boyfriend. I lost track of the time."

Charles was a bi-sexual co-worker of Annie's at the health clinic where she worked as an X-ray technician. I'd never met him before, but always enjoyed the tales Annie would tell me about him.

"WARRIOR POSE," instructed Paula.

And although I'd enjoy her stories about Charles, I was hoping she'd wait to tell me after class so I could concentrate on my yoga work. But, that of course, would be like wishing for snow on a ninety-five degree day.

"So, anyway," she continued murmuring while gracefully flexing her one knee, "Charles was seeing this guy for about six months and things were getting hot and heavy. Until he stopped by unannounced at his lover's place last night to find him giving it up the ass to a seventeen-year-old boy. And I thought I had problems....."

"SEATED FORWARD BEND!"

"So Mags, anything interesting going on in your office this week?"

"Not really," I grimaced as I tried to hold my pose. "Except for this morning. I had a pretty unique visitor."

"Yeah?" Annie's eyes brightened. "Do tell!"

"Well, this guy came in who lives the life of a gigolo shacking up with sugar mamas. As a matter of fact, he's living with an extremely powerful and wealthy middle-aged woman right now. And he came to ask me to help him learn how to fall in love."

"Are you serious?" Annie giggled as Paula passed us a warning look. "How do you teach someone to fall in love?"

I lowered my voice further so that I would be audible only to Annie. "There are ways. I haven't mapped them all out in his case yet, but there are actual steps that you go through when you fall in love with a person."

"Yeah, three of them," Annie snickered. "Step one is boy meets girl. Step two is boy takes off girl's clothes, as well as his own. And we all know what step three is..."

I rolled my eyes. "Love is much more complex than that. I just hope I do a great job with this guy. He's got plenty of connections with old money and, if I can get in good with him, maybe he can hook me up with some potential clients for Greg. If that happens, I'd be over the moon."

"TRIANGLE POSE!"

"I hate this damn pose," I bitched while contorting my body into twisted taffy. "We'll talk later, Annie."

"Oh! Before I forget to tell you later," she breathed with ease, "Mom is coming in on the train Saturday night for the shower on Sunday and she is going to have to stay with you overnight."

"What? Are you crazy? I told you that Greg and I are celebrating our wedding anniversary this weekend."

"Yes, I know. But you wouldn't want Mom to have to stay at a hotel, now, would you?"

"What's wrong with her staying with you?" I grunted.

"I'm probably gonna have a date that night," she purred.

"With who?"

"Oh, probably with the hot guy in the red trunks three rows behind us who hasn't been able to take his eyes off my ass since this class started."

CHAPTER FOUR

"**H**ere's to enduring another seven year itch," toasted my husband, as we clinked our glasses of Pinot Grigio, feeling buzzed at our secluded, corner table at Affamato Cucina. This swank Italian restaurant, located in Center City, was a favorite of Greg's and mine, so I decided it would be a wonderful place to celebrate our anniversary.

I took a swallow of my wine. "I don't make you too itchy, now do I?"

Greg's face crinkled. "Incredibly itchy. Like poison ivy."

From the moment I had laid eyes on him back in high-school, I knew I had met someone special. I had just moved to Pennsylvania from New Jersey with mom and Annie a few years after dad died, and was nervous about starting my first day at Abington Senior High midway through the second semester. Greg was sitting behind me in my history class and tapped me on the shoulder to ask to borrow a pencil. The instant I saw the sparkle in his deep-set, dark brown eyes, I knew I had found my first friend in my new hometown. Not only had I found just a friend, but my best friend. We were pretty much inseparable during our high-school years. We took a mutual break from each other for a year or so while we were away at college; we both felt it would be good for us to date other people. But, as fate would have it, we knew we were made for each other and married a few months after graduation. We remained very close... until recently.

"Finally! It's so nice to get some quality time to spend together. I feel like I hardly get to see you anymore."

"Hun, you know how difficult it is for me to find free time right now. Ever since Carlson resigned and I filled his shoes, the workload for me has just piled up. Believe me, I'm doing the best I can do."

"Why did Carlson resign, anyway? Too heavy a workload?"

Greg laughed. "No, he was caught with his pants down in the file room with the girl that operates the phone lines."

"No shit. You mean that girl who answers the phone with the British accent?"

"Yep. That's the one."

"And what happened to her?"

"I'm not exactly sure. She quit or got fired or something. But Carlson left with things being a total mess. It's just gonna take some time to get adjusted and clean up some of the bullshit. But, don't worry, things will settle down a bit."

"Ha," I snickered. "I've heard that one before. Like about five months
ago."

"Mags, you know how the market gets! It can be really unpredictable. I have to constantly be on top of things or I'm in a lot of hot water with a lot of big people."

"I know," I moaned as our waitress delivered our Caesar salads. "It's just that... I miss you. I miss us. It's important for us to find more quality time to put into our relationship. If we don't put some effort into nurturing it, our relationship together may suffer."

I slid my hand atop of if his. "And I don't want to lose what we've got together. I hate feeling disconnected from you."

I could feel the warmth in Greg's eyes, but could also see the frustration. "Maggie, please. I told you I am doing the best I can. All this hard work I'm doing, I'm doing for us. I'm doing it for our son. I'm doing the best I can for our family's future by investing in some hard work now so that one day we can send Derek off to college with his tuition fully paid. Then, maybe, I can look into an early retirement so I can spend all of my free quality time with my wonderful wife."

"Is that what our plan is?"

"Have you got a better one?"

I thought for a moment, pushing my fork heedlessly among the limp Romaine leaves on my plate. "I don't know. I was kind of hoping maybe you'd want another child."

Lately, I yearned to add another addition to our family. I secretly

32

desired another child, a sibling for Derek. But, not just for Derek, who was getting older, but a little someone else around who depended on me. I liked feeling needed.

Greg took a long sip of wine, washing down the salad he instantaneously devoured. "Maggie, I thought we talked about this already. You know how I feel about that."

Of course I did. I was just hoping maybe he'd changed his mind a bit. I first brought the idea to him a year or so ago. I had hit my mid-thirties and thought if I'd wanted another child, I should start planning for it. In the back of my heart, I'd always wished that one day I would have a little girl, so I quizzed Greg on the notion. To my surprise, Greg frowned on the idea. He was a wonderful father and had such a great relationship with Derek, I couldn't imagine that he wouldn't go for the idea of having another little one around. He claimed it would be silly to have another child, after already having halfway reared our son. He had compared it to starting a halfway completed project all over again from the beginning, and then protested highly against disrupting and delaying the future years we'd get to spend together child-care free. When I tried to push the issue that I did not want Derek to be an only child, Greg countered with the fact that Derek had twenty-two cousins that lived within a ten-mile radius of our home who he spent much time with.

"Maggie, if you want something else to take care of so badly, why don't we just get a dog?"

I frowned. "No way, Greg! Do you know what a pain in the ass it would be to take care of a damn dog? And how in the world can you compare a dog to having another baby?"

"I don't know," he responded, as our main cuisine arrived. "But I'll bet if you ask Derek which one he'd want, he'd say he rather have the dog."

After some dessert and a little slow-dancing, Greg and I were ready to make our way home. When we got inside our charcoal BMW, Greg leaned over and popped open the glove compartment, carefully removing a small box.

"I forgot to bring this inside the restaurant," he said, handing me the box. "Happy Anniversary, Mrs. Simmons."

Enthralled, I quickly opened the tiny box and gasped upon seeing its contents.

"Oh, my God, Greg! They're beautiful!" I cried, pulling out a pair of genuine cultured pearl earrings surrounded by tiny glistening bursts of diamonds and blue sapphires.

"I had them made especially for you. I want you to wear them everyday so you can think of me when I can't be with you."

I removed the silver hoops from my ears and eagerly placed in my new gems. "How do they look?"

"Beautiful," Greg smiled. "But not half as beautiful as you."

"I love you," I moaned, leaning in to kiss my wondrous husband.

Fortunately, when we arrived home that night, Derek was asleep in bed and I took a quick peek into the guest bedroom to find my mother asleep as well. Annie had dropped Mom off earlier that evening, from the train station, shortly after Greg and I ventured off to dinner. As for the rest of the evening, my husband and I found ourselves in bed, quietly making slow and passionate love.

The next morning seemed to arrive within seconds of the night before. I felt as though I had only slept a mere three minutes when I awakened to the sounds of sizzling bacon accompanied by my mother's humming voice. I could smell the scent of strongly brewed coffee and pictured my mother's trademark jitters that would arise within her after she drank a couple cups of her bitter home brew. And just then, I remembered the bridal shower.

Shit, I thought as I read the clock on the bedside table - 10:17 a.m.. I wobbled my way into the shower and stood motionless inside the stall. I allowed the pulsating stream of water to caress my body while I mentally recollected the magnificent evening I had just spent with Greg. My pleasant thoughts were interrupted by a loud knock on the door.

"Christ, Maggie. I was wondering if you were ever gonna wake up!"

"Hello to you, too, Ma!" I yelled from behind the shower curtain. "Do you need something right now?"

"I wanted to know what you wanted for breakfast this morning. I made up some bacon already. How do you want me to make your eggs?"

"Scrambled. Dry. Thank you!"

When I arrived back into my bedroom after my shower, I noticed my husband, who was sleeping buck naked on top of the sheets before I got in the shower, was clothed with a tee-shirt and shorts. He popped an eye open while I was slipping on my chemise.

He mumbled. "Mag, could you please have a talk with your mother one of these days about maybe knocking on our bedroom door before entering it? And, if she chooses not to do so, entering will be at her own risk!"

I passed through the living room on my way to the kitchen and caught a glimpse of my son lying in front of the television, propped up on a pillow with a joystick glued to his hand.

"Good morning, Sweetheart. Did you eat yet?"

"Yep. Grandma fed me about an hour ago. Is Dad up yet?"

"Just about," I answered.

"Cool," he replied.

When I arrived in the kitchen, the smell of the coffee magnified, as was the stench of my mother's Jean Nate. Annie and I swore she bathed in that stuff. Mom looked pretty though, dressed in a pastel floral linen pantsuit that spoke earnestly of style and comfort. She wore her hair in a smooth bob, but it looked as though there was a hair color circus going on in it so I couldn't tell you if she'd be considered a blonde, brunette, or redhead. She was a petite 5'4", and at fifty-eight years of age, she could still pass easily for a woman of forty-five.

"Maggie, honey, come here and give me a hug," she demanded while dropping her spatula.

I gave my mom a quick hug and noticed instantly that there felt less of her. "Mom, did you lose weight?"

"Yeah, a few pounds," she laughed nonchalantly. "Now I can probably share clothes with both of my daughters if I hem them a bit."

"You look good, Mom," I smiled. "But don't lose anymore. You are tiny enough as it is."

We headed to the dining room table with our breakfasts in hand, trying to catch up on things since we last saw each other four months ago. Mom had moved to Manhattan six years earlier to live with a man she was dating, named Oliver. Oliver and Mom lived together for one year and decided that co-habitation wasn't going to work out for them. Since Mom had found such a great job at a big publishing company, she decided to stay in Manhattan for awhile. Somewhere along the road, Mom and Oliver ended up back with each other, but resided in separate apartments.

"Ollie and I saw a great movie the other night called 'The Sixth Sense'. They filmed it right here in Philadelphia. Have you seen it yet?"

"No, I haven't been to the movies lately, Ma. Derek and I usually have a hard time agreeing on a film these days and Greg hasn't had much time for me lately with his work and all."

"Aw," Mom cooed. "Did you have a nice time last night for your anniversary, Dear?"

"Yes. And Greg got me these," I smiled while showing off my new ear gems.

"They're beautiful! Greg is a wonderful man," Mom chanted with glee. "And I think it's wonderful that even though his schedule has been hectic lately, he's been able to find the time to take Derek to the amusement park today."

I nearly choked on my bacon. "What?"

Mom blinked excessively. "Oh my, I hope I didn't say anything I wasn't supposed to. But Derek mentioned this morning about heading out to Great Adventure with his dad today."

I had to admit, I was a little irate at hearing that. I'd been bugging Greg all season to pick a date for our annual trip to the amusement park. He'd always told me that he was too busy at the time to plan such a thing. He knew how much I loved going and spending the day as a family, and loved feeling that wild adrenaline rush on the roller coasters or getting drenched on the log-flume rides. So, why on earth would he plan this trip on a day I was busy and then not even mention it to me? "Derek! Come here for a minute!"

"What's the matter, Mom?" Derek asked while strolling his way into the dining room.

"Did you tell Grandma that you and Dad were going to Great Adventure today?"

My son's hazel eyes, which were just like my mothers', filled with sudden dread. He looked over at my mother as if to seek solace for the explanation he would have to give.

"Yea," he spoke in a low tone. "But it was supposed to be a secret. Dad didn't want me to tell you about it. He said you'd get upset because you wouldn't be able to go with us today."

"Well, I am kind of upset," I told him. "I would've liked to go. It should be the three of us as a family going, like we usually do."

I could tell Derek was getting upset, feeling like he was torn.

"I'm sorry, Mom, I'd love it if you could come, too. Dad said it could be like a father and son day for us. Just the guys. Please don't tell him I told you about it. I don't want him to get mad at me and not take me at all."

I sighed. "Okay, my buddy, I won't say a word. Just promise me you'll be careful. And if you have any problems, call me on my cell phone."

"Thanks Mom!" he smiled as he slid back to playing his video

37

games.

"He is such a sweet boy, and getting so big!" Mom exclaimed. "I'm sure all the girls at school will be chasing that handsome little devil soon."

"Yeah," I smiled, "but he'll always be my baby."

Mom grinned in accordance. "Yes. They always stay that way. Speaking of which, where the hell is my baby Annie?"

Annie arrived at my house a good twenty minutes late, which was typical Annie style, and in a tizzy as well. Mom and I hopped in her Buick, me in front and Mom in back, and she sped off frantically as though trying to make-up for the twenty minutes she had lost.

"How was your date last night?" I asked her.

"Totally hot," she beamed.

"Will you be going out with him again?"

"Hmpff," Annie thought, "I'm not sure."

Mom laughed. "Annie, you just said the guy you went out with was totally hot. Well, if you thought that, why wouldn't you want to see him again? Was he a nice man?"

Annie gave me a knowing side-glance. "Well, Ma, let's just say at least his body was totally hot."

"Annie Von Worth!" Mom's voice rose with disgust. "You didn't go and sleep with that man on the first date now did you?"

"Ma!" Annie shrieked, embarrassed.

"You girls today have no shame," Mom rambled, "If you sleep with a man right away, they'll never have any respect for you. He'll treat you like a slut."

"Mom, it doesn't matter if I sleep with him the first night or the fortieth night, a guy doesn't respect me either way. So, I might as well sleep with him whenever I feel like it so I can at least get something out of it before he decides to move on to the next whore."

THE CARDHOLDER

The Von Worth girls. It was always interesting when the three of us would get together. We bickered a lot, but always remained close. For a time, the three of us is all we had for a family. Patricia, or Pat, as my mother liked to be called, had been adopted and ran away from home when she was seventeen. When she was nineteen, she met my father, a man I only know of by the name Neil. She married him at age twenty, and gave birth to me a year later. One night, when I was two years old, my mother came home from the market to find a note my father left on the dresser table explaining that he needed a change in his life. He had left us that evening. And never came back.

Mom worked hard to support the two of us, and eventually found a good secretarial job with a law firm. There she met and fell in love with a wonderful, handsome man named Nikolas Von Worth. Mom and Nikolas married, and Nikolas adopted me as his own daughter. I finally had a father of my very own, who showed me so much love and adoration. A few years later, when I was seven, Annie popped into the picture. We were a very happy family, and I have many pleasant memories from that period in my life. All that changed one evening.

One night, when I was twelve, I came home from studying at a neighbor's house. As soon as I walked in the door, Mom yelled to me from the bathroom to go and find Annie and bring her in for her bath. I looked in her room and couldn't find her. I called out to her, but she did not reply. As I stood in the hallway, I heard her little voice coming from Dad's study. I pushed open the slightly ajar door of the room to find Annie, who was about five at the time, perched on Dad's lap with her favorite stuffed bunny rabbit, named Petey, in hand. Dad's head was slumped over to the side and his face was an ash gray color. Annie was playing with the rabbit, talking to it, and then to Daddy, asking that he please wake up and play with them. I cried out to Mom. Dad had apparently suffered a heart attack and died instantly. I'll never forget when the men dressed in white came and went inside the room to remove his body. Little Annie cried out hysterically, kicking and screaming at the men as they tried to pry her away from Dad's lifeless body. I'll never forget that moment. I'm sure Mom and Annie won't either. Mom never remarried after Dad, claiming she could never love a man the way she loved him. To this day, I believe that was true.

When we arrived at Trista's bridal shower, held at her mother's house, all the other guests had already arrived. Mom quickly put herself to work in Mrs. Bellow's kitchen and the two moms chit-chatted away as they worked the final prepping on the finger foods. Annie and I headed out back to a large, paper mache decorated deck, where the shower itself was to take place. We greeted a couple of guests moments before Trista arrived.

I was never too fond of Annie's friends, especially Trista. I felt they were quite snobbish and selfish with certain things when it came to Annie. Annie was a good friend, always there when somebody needed her, and she always put the needs of her friends before her own. They, on the other hand, were self-centered, thinking only of themselves and would only seem to bother with Annie if it was something for their own benefit. I tried pointing that out to Annie on several distinct occasions, but she would do nothing but defend her so-called comrades, blinded by an intricate mix of naivety, disbelief and loyalty.

Trista, who had an unnatural dark tan look for someone who was fair-skinned, was quick to absorb all the attention donned on her. Annie was to be the maid-of-honor at her wedding, which was to take place in early October. However, Trista changed her mind in early July, requesting that their friend, Natalie, take Annie's place. Annie was devastated, but took the news like a champ, hiding her crestfallen pain behind her Grace Kelly smile. I, on the other hand, was outraged by Trista's utter shallowness.

"So, Annie, have you found anyone to bring as a guest to my wedding?" Trista asked, while unwrapping her second crock-pot.

"No. Kinda going through a dry spell right now with guys. But I did hook-up with this really good-looking hunk last night."

"Oh, that's nice," Trista remarked with a touch of arrogance in her catty voice. "I remember those days. They seem so silly to me now that I have Glen in my life. You gotta settle down one of these days, Annie, or one day you'll just wake up an old maid!"

Some of the guests let out mocking laughs.

Annie made no attempt to defend herself, so I did it for her. "Well, you know, Trista, if you were as beautiful as Annie is, you'd realize that it's pretty difficult to choose just one man when there are so many lying at your feet. Something like that takes time."

Annie gave me a glance of thanks and I suddenly realized why she asked me to attend. She merely wanted a true friend by her side.

After the gift unwrapping was completed, a group of five or so women huddled by the dessert table. They were passing pictures around amongst each other. Trista, Annie, and I busied ourselves with piling up the gifts and gathering bits of wrappings when one of the women called out, "Hey Trista! Come over here! We got the pictures back from Sam and Dina's wedding last week."

"Wha... What?" Annie questioned, despair choking her voice. "Did somebody just say that Sam and Dina got married? My Sam?"

Hearing that news was equivalent to hearing a bomb drop for Annie, and I felt her shock waves. Sam was Annie's first and last true love. They dated several years ago and were totally smitten with each other. The problem was that Sam's friend Jay had the hots for Annie as well, and Sam knew that. And so did some of their mutual friends, which included a girl named Dina, who had the hots for Sam. In a ploy to get Sam and Annie to split up, Jay had gotten Annie smashing drunk one night at a pub, while she was awaiting Sam's arrival from work, and Jay took her home with him. In the meantime, Dina "conveniently" ran into Sam, and told him a story of Annie's torrid affair with Jay. Disbelieving Dina, but needing to see it for himself, Sam went directly to Jay's house, where he found Annie lying asleep naked in his bedroom.

Sam and Annie broke up after the incident; Sam believing that Annie had been unfaithful to him, which had broken his heart. He truly

41

loved her, as Annie did him. It was rumored that Sam and Dina had moved in together shortly thereafter and after several tries to get back in touch with Sam, Annie was left at a dead end. No new phone number and no new address. Even his place of employment had changed. She relied, over the years, on the mutual friends that she shared with both Sam and Dina, to help her in her search for him. They all said they did not know of Sam's whereabouts, but I felt that they did and kept close-mouthed about it, believing the tale that Annie was, in fact, a slut. Annie believed in her heart that she and Sam would cross paths again and be reunited in their undying love. In an instant, the hope-filled dream she had been clinging to had been destroyed for her.

The ensemble of women deadened their voices, looking at each other for the one that would break the silence and give an answer to Annie's inquiry. None of them were brave enough to disclose any words to try and pacify the grief-stricken look Annie wore on her face.

"Natalie? Amy? Trista? Did you all know that Sam was getting married last week? Did all of you go to the wedding, too?"

The guilty looks on the girls' faces answered her.

Annie let out a strangled cry. "How could you? You guys knew all this time about Sam's whereabouts and you've never told me? You all knew how I felt about him and you've kept him a secret from me! How can any of you call me your friend? Friends don't do that. They stick together. No matter what."

"Annie, don't take any of this personally," Natalie spoke up, "but Dina is our friend, too. And we have to respect her wishes as..."

"Oh fuck off Natalie," hissed Annie, "You're nothing but a friggin' brown-noser and a phony two-faced bitch. Just like that good for nothing Dina. Sam loved me! Not her! And all of you bitches know that!"

Humiliated, Annie trotted along to the side of the house and disappeared. I gave her a moment, then followed her steps to deliver some much needed comfort. I found her on the porch steps of the house cranking on her lighter to light the cigarette that dangled on the edge of her lips. A single tear trickled down her cheek as she swore repeatedly at her defective lighter.

"Hey you," I approached with feather weight footsteps, sitting beside her and taking the lighter from her hand. I popped on a flame with one flick of my thumb and placed it atop of Annie's cigarette. She sucked deeply from it.

"I thought you quit."

"Please don't lecture me now, Mags."

I placed my hand on her arm. "Are you okay, Honey?"

Annie looked at me, eyes welling up with more tears. I grabbed my little sister and hugged her tight. She began to wail like a helpless baby and fought hard to calm herself.

"I can't believe what I just heard," she whimpered. "I can't believe my own friends could be so sneaky and hide a fact from me that they knew meant so much to me. Why would they do that to me?"

I let go of my embrace and placed my hands on Annie's cheeks, wiping the wetness from them. "Annie, I've told you before about your so-called friends. They don't care about you. They're phonies and only care about themselves."

"Yeah, but Trista? She's supposed to be my best friend! I've known her since high-school."

"Trista is self-centered, too, as far as I'm concerned. She's always been jealous of you, Annie. I've seen it over the years in the way she'd talk to you or treat you. It's nothing you've ever done to provoke it, that's just how she is. And believe me, Sweetie, I know what I'm talking about. After all, analyzing human nature is my profession."

"But, it doesn't make sense. Why would she be jealous of me?"

"Because you have something that she does not."

"Like what?"

"A little something called moxie! And, Annie, baby, you've got plenty of it!"

"Oh stop, Mags. You're just saying that because I'm your sister."

"No I'm not! How many people do you know, besides yourself, who can make jaws drop when entering a room?"

A faint smile grew upon Annie's rosebud lips.

I continued. "And how many times have you gone out with Trista and your other friends to have the bulk of, if not all the men coming onto you? They're jealous of all the attention you get!"

Her grin widened. "True. I guess I do have more of that moxie stuff than them. So, they can kiss my ass!"

"That's right. God, I remember back when Greg and I were in high school and we pulled into the driveway at Mom's house after school to find you, I think you were eleven years old at the time, hiding behind the shed with like four or five boys having a kissing contest. I could have died! And I remember Greg telling me, 'Maggie, you better keep your eye on that little Annie. She's gonna be a real heart breaker when she gets older.'"

Her newly formed smile slowly diminished. "But, about Sam. I can't believe he married Dina. He couldn't even stand her when I was with him. How could he marry her? He was supposed to marry me."

"Well, Annie, God works in funny ways. Maybe he just wasn't the one for you."

Annie kicked off her heels and placed them in her hands. "But, Mags, you don't understand. I loved Sam so much. I'll never find another love like that again. Ever. You don't know what it's like out there. You've been spoiled by having Greg in your life for so long."

Her face suddenly crinkled. "Hey! Speaking of which, how did your anniversary dinner go last night?"

"Good," I responded pulling my tresses away from my ears. "Greg got me these earrings for a gift."

"They're beautiful!" Annie beamed. "I must confess, though. I did help him pick them out. He stressed to me that he wanted something with blue sapphires. So, I chose a pair that was spiced up a bit with diamonds. Do you like them?"

"Love them. Thanks. You did a great job."

"Well, he did tell me to pick out something that was one-of-a-kind. You wouldn't believe the bucks he shelled out for those. You'll have to give him head every night of the week for months to thank him for those babies."

"Well, I wouldn't mind a little more action between the sheets from him to tell you the truth. He's been sparse in that department lately. I was lucky to get something from him last night."

"How come? What do you think it is? Is he becoming impotent or something?"

"I don't know," I replied. "It might be because of his job stress. Or maybe he's a little afraid because I have been mentioning to him lately that I'd like to have another child."

"Is he okay with that yet?"

I sighed. "No, he's still not interested in having another kid."

"So what?" Annie shrugged. "Why don't you go ahead and get pregnant anyway? I'm sure once the baby gets here he'll be psyched about it."

"No, that's where you're wrong. Greg and I have a strict rule about trust in our relationship. If I were to go behind his back, and deliberately get pregnant knowing his position on the matter, it would break our trust in each other. We've always said if our trust in each other is ever broken, our relationship together would be ruined."

A red sports car roared out of nowhere and pulled into the driveway of the Bellows residence. A man emerged from the vehicle and headed towards Annie and me.

"Good afternoon, ladies," he spoke, nodding his head. "So, how are things with the shower wrapping up?"

Annie and I gave each other a knowing look.

"Oh, just fine," Annie replied.

"Hey, I remember you. Your name is Annie, right?" said the man.

"Yep, that's me."

"I'm Glen. Trista's fiancee. You remember me, right? That night out at Drew's Pub on Main Street?"

"Yeah," Annie smiled. "I remember you! Of course, I had only met you once before. We had fun that night."

"Oh, we had a blast that night, didn't we? So... how come I haven't seen you around in a while? How come you don't ever come over and visit us? I always tell Trista 'Hey, why don't you call your friend Annie and have her hang out with us sometime?' She tells me every time she calls you that you say you're busy. What's the matter? Don't you like us or something?"

Annie's face filled with disgust. "Funny. Every time I talk to Trista, she's told me that you guys were too busy to get together with me."

Glen's face fell. "Oh. Wow. Okay. Maybe I'd better get inside. Take care, ladies."

Annie growled. "I need to get out of here. Mags, are you ready to leave this friggin' place?"

"Yes," I answered, the mere thought filling my mind with a happy vibe. "But there's just one problem. One of us has to go in there and try to pull Mom away from helping out Mrs. Bellows in the kitchen."

CHAPTER FIVE

Monday morning snuck back into my life and although it was a day I traditionally hated, soon it would become a day I looked forward to. That is after I wrapped up my sessions with Sue Adelsberg, of course. On this particular Monday, Sue had managed to coerce her husband, Harry, into accompanying her. I had met the miserable bastard before, and his narrow-minded disposition seemed unchanged.

"You psychologists are good for shit," he sneered. "All you do is make people rehash a bunch of bull and hit them with a huge bill when their time is up. You doctors don't give a rat's ass about us common people. You just want to make your big money by sitting there listening to other people's problems and if your patient doesn't have a problem, you'll find one for them to have so they'll have to keep comin' back to see you again so you can get paid even more! You're nothin' but thieves in my book. I don't know what the hell I'm even here for. I don't have a problem with anything. But it seems as though you've made my wife think I have one!"

"Mr. Adelsberg, please calm yourself down. You have a right to your opinions, but please have some common decency and show some respect while in my office. I appreciate your coming here today on behalf of Sue's wishes. I don't know if you are aware of it or not, but your wife is becoming very unhappy in your marriage."

"I don't want to talk about that stuff here. That is personal information between me and my wife. It's none of your business."

Sue spoke up. "It is her business, Harry! I've tried to talk to you about how I've been feeling and you always tell me you don't wanna talk about it. Well, I need to talk about it or I'm gonna explode! Dr.

Simmons has been wonderful to me and has helped me out so much. But, I'm only half of our marriage and if you don't want to put any effort into it on your part, I don't know what is going to happen."

"Calm down, Susie dear, there is no need for you to keep makin' mountains out of molehills."

Sue lashed out wildly at Harry. "How dare you say that to me! Don't you love me?"

"Of course I do! You know that!"

"Well, you hardly ever say it."

"I say it," he expressed, clearly embarrassed. "But how many damn times do you want me to say it? Nothing's ever good enough for you. If I said it ten times, you'd want me to say it twenty. If I said it a hundred times, you'd want a thousand. When does it end?"

"It's not supposed to end! You fool! That's what a marriage is about! It's for forever! Not just for the wedding night!"

With their arms folded, both Harry and Sue remained quiet for a moment, with just the sounds of their quick breaths rushing in and out of their flared nostrils. Harry then gazed over at me. "Okay, Doc, you win. I'll let you help us. Just none of that men are from Mars and women are from Venus shit, you got me?"

I smiled and gave a wink. "Deal."

Upon wrapping up my session with the Adelsbergs, I walked them to Sandy's desk and requested that Harry return with Sue the following week. He reluctantly indicated he would try. I had the feeling he would be the new thorn in my side to start off the week, his bull-headedness replacing his wife's whining.

"Who's my next appointment, Sandy? Is it that Mickey Dillon guy?"

"Yes, Maggie. He is here now. Just stepped outside for a smoke."

"Send him in when he comes back inside, okay?"

When I arrived back inside my office, I pulled out the skinny file I had on Mick Dillon. I had thought about him from time to time during this past week, still in awe of the specific purpose why this mysterious man set out to look for my help. It was quite unique to come across a young, handsome man who desperately sought out to fall completely and deeply in love with a woman. I usually found myself helping out at the other end of the spectrum; prying into the delicate emotions of lovesick women hurt by men like him. I made a swift realization that this task would be a good change of focus for me. Never, of course, realizing the torrid effect it would bring about in my life.

"Good morning, Dr. Simmons," he said, seated before me.

"Good morning, Mick. How are things with you today?"

"Okay, I guess," he replied with a touch of drowsiness in his voice. "I'm just a little tired. Got out of work a little later than usual this morning."

"Oh. Where do you work?"

"Mason Pierce Hotel. You know, down on City Line Avenue."

I was astounded. "Really? That is quite a prestigious establishment. What is it that you do there?"

"Tend bar," he replied with a sloppy grin. "I usually get out of work by three a.m., but some of the Seventy-Sixers were hanging out in the lounge area, so I stayed a bit longer. Have you ever been there?"

I nodded. "Yes, I've been to several conferences hosted there. It's a marvelous place."

"I'm sorry, Mick," I added, somewhat confused, "but, I didn't realize you still worked at bartending. You gave me the impression last week that you did not need to work because you were... pardon the phrase... a kept man."

"Sure. I'm that, too. But, how do you think I meet my monetary mommas?"

I could've easily been bothered by a remark like that; coming from a greedy leech who preyed upon another's wealth for their own personal benefit. But, for some reason, I didn't get that leeching vibe from Mick. He had a sweet, innocent, captivating demeanor about him that kept me from feeling anything negative towards him. I tried to keep myself wise to that notion, but easily fell victim to the vulnerability that spoke within his eyes.

"Is that how you met Alexis?"

"Yeah, I met Alexis about six months ago when they held a DOW fundraiser at the hotel."

"DOW?"

"Defenders of Wildlife Association. Alex is a board member of the group. I'll never forget the moment I laid eyes on her. She wore this real sexy little black dress, and her blonde hair was piled on top of her head. She came over to my counter and asked for Jack Daniels on the rocks. I commented to her how I thought it was such a ballsy drink for a feminine woman like herself. We got to talking, both of us being animal lovers and all. She told me about her two dogs and her cat. She spoke so passionately about them, and I remarked on how much I'd love to meet them one day. She took me home that night."

"How would you describe your relationship with Alex?"

Mick's face displayed a warm expression of emotion. "Alex is a very special woman. She's got integrity, depth, strength. Everything about her is alluring. She has real sex appeal."

"Well," I retorted, "She does sound like an amazing person. But, you haven't exactly answered the question I asked you. Mick, how would you describe your relationship with Alex?"

Mick subjected himself to deep thought and I could tell he felt distraught.

"Alex and I have a good relationship. As good as it can be, I guess."

"Meaning what, exactly?"

"Meaning exactly that. It's as good as it can get with her."

"Hmmmpf," I paused. "It's as good as it can get with her. Mick, I'm going to ask you to do a little something for me. I want you to draw me a couple pictures. Not the type of pictures you make with paint, but the type of picture you can make using words. Now, for picture number one, I want you to re-create a photo of your relationship with Alex. And in picture number two, I want you to draw me a photo of the relationship you want to have with a woman. You understand?"

He seemed eager to fulfill my curious endeavor, taking his time carefully preparing his words. "My relationship with Alex is... friendship and sex. It's nothing more than that. The relationship I want with a woman is... pure passion. Constant passion. It's wanting to be with that person constantly and her constantly wanting to be with me."

"So, you're looking for your soul mate."

Mick let out a gentle laugh. "No, not exactly. I don't believe in soul mates. I don't believe that there is only one person out in the world exactly meant for another. I do believe that certain people are meant to be together at certain times in their lives."

"Then that would make you opposed to the revelries of marriage, now wouldn't it?"

He nodded. "I guess it would in a way."

"Mick, you've got me a little confused here. You came to me asking for my help so you could learn how to fall in love. Yet, if you fell in love with someone, you'd feel as though it should be a temporary thing?"

His eyes grew large. "No, I don't want you to misunderstand me here. Let me explain myself a little better to you. What I want, I'm sure, is the same thing you probably hear all the time from people. I want to experience what it's like to fall deeply in love with a woman. I want to know what it's like to feel her every breath inside my own body. I want our bodies to feel that electrifying jolt every time we touch. I want to know her every thought and desire. I want her to feel mine. To share that similar longing for each other. Pure raw desire... pure uninhibited passion."

I became speechless, momentarily seized by the power of his words.

"And I'm not saying that I'm opposed to the thought of getting married. I'd also love to become a father one day. I'd really love to have a daughter of my own. There's something really special about a little girl. Don't you think so, Dr. Simmons?"

"Yes, I think so," I replied, startled.

Mick sat up in his chair, leaning in towards my desk. "Yea, I'd like to do the family thing. Go to the ballgames, go fishing, or my personal favorite, hitting the amusement parks. It must be fun to go on those roller-coaster rides and the log- flumes when you have your own kids to go on them with you."

Mick looked deep into my eyes and his dialogue was hitting strangely close to home with me. I disliked it and found it eerie, so I quickly reverted back to our previous conversation.

"Okay. Let's get back to the soul mate thing because I'd hate to see someone fall in love believing it could not last."

"Love can't last. It's only a temporary thing for the time it was meant for."

"Love is a choice, Mick. It will only last as long as both parties wish for it to be. Staying in love requires constant nurturing. True love has the possibility to last forever."

"That's where you're wrong, Dr. Simmons. A person does not have control of their own emotions. We can't choose how we feel about anybody. People change. Feelings change. How can you promise to love somebody forever when you can't control what your feelings are destined for?"

Mick posed a legitimate argument onto my sentiment. I knew this would require intense research on my part to properly convey the professional service Mick sought from me. After our session ended, I asked Mick to stop at the bookstore on his way home to pick up THE PATH TO LOVE by Deepak Chopra, to use as a guide between our sessions.

I had been a fan of Deepak's teachings and went out west once to attend one of his seminars. When it comes to human nature, he is a brilliant man and full of insightful, thought-provoking wisdom. I owned several of his books and have referred to them often in specific situations I've had with my patients. THE PATH TO LOVE had Mickey Dillon written all over it.

THE CARDHOLDER

When I arrived home from work that evening, I went directly upstairs to my bedroom closet to search for my own copy of the book. I stepped into my walk-in closet and reached up to get the box of books that sat upon the shelf. A small, black case, which was sitting on the box of books, fell by my side. Not recognizing the box, I pried it open. That's when I first laid eyes on that damn gun.

CHAPTER SIX

"Greg! Get up here right now!" I yelled upon hearing the front door open after my husband's car pulled into the driveway. Moments before, I stood in the kitchen preparing a quick meal of hot dogs and macaroni and cheese, ill at ease at the thought that a lethal weapon occupied a space under my roof. Now I stood at my closet doorway, dressed in my gear and ablaze with anger.

"What's the matter?" he had the nerve to ask.

"What's the matter?" I snapped in a sarcastic tone. "I'll tell you what's the matter. Since when did we decide to keep a gun in our house?"

Greg's face exhibited a combination of shock, guilt, and anger. "I was afraid you'd come across that. I should've hid it a little better from you."

"What? Are you kidding me? What in the world are you doing with one of those things in my house? Are you in some sort of trouble or something?"

"No, it's nothing like that," he replied while plopping on the bed to remove his shoes. "I got it for protection. That's all."

"Protection? Protection from what?"

"I don't know, like a burglar or something. Have you seen the news lately? People are getting robbed all the time. If someone breaks into my home, I want to be able to protect my family. Is that too much to ask?"

"Jesus, Greg! You want to protect your family? We have a twelve-year-old boy in this house for Christ's sake! I know there have been reports of robberies in the news lately. But there are just as many reports about these kids finding guns in their home that accidentally go off and kill somebody. Is that what you call protecting your family?"

"I knew you'd be against it, Maggie," Greg spoke with frustration while loosening his tie. "That's why I never mentioned a word about it to you. I just knew you would freak out."

I was furious. "You're damned right I'm freaked out about it. And I want you to get rid of it. It's too dangerous to have around."

"Oh, c'mon. You're being ridiculous."

"I don't think I am! I feel very uncomfortable with that thing in here, and what would happen if our son or any of his friends got a hold of it?"

"Maggie, would you relax? First of all, that gun has been in this house for four months already and if you hadn't come across it today, you'd have never known it was here. And secondly, I know my son pretty well, well enough to know that he'd never go routing through his parent's closet out of sheer boredom. The gun stays. It's staying in the closet. End of story."

I found it very difficult to concentrate at the yoga class that evening. I was consumed by the image of my husband entering a gun shop and purchasing that nasty little pistol. We had an alarm system at home so I could not understand what would spark the need in Greg to want to buy a gun. I thought of mentioning the episode to Annie, but quickly realized she'd tell Mom, so I kept my mouth shut. Besides, Annie was too preoccupied with who was staring at her ass that evening.

After my yoga class, I stopped at the supermarket to pick up a couple of items, which ended up filling up about four grocery bags. I pulled into the driveway, grabbed two of the bags and I proceeded into the house, looking to see if either Greg or Derek was around to grab the other two still in the car. I heard them shooting pool in the basement so I didn't want to disturb them.

I headed back to the car and as I closed the car door, after retrieving my final bags, I was startled. Alexis LeNoir stood in front of me with a leash dangling in one hand that was attached to her toy poodle's neck. She was just as beautiful as everyone described her to be. I could also see Jill Coopersmith in the background; the newsy neighborhood gnat was peeping through her window at us.

Alexis grinned at me. "Good evening, Dr. Simmons. I want to thank you for offering to help out my Mickey. And if you do a good job of helping him, I'll certainly return the favor and do a good job of generously helping out you and your husband."

Upon having spoken those words, Alexis turned and walked away. I'd not been given the chance to get out a word of my own, left to wonder what she meant by what she had said. That was the first and last time I had met the mystifying woman.

CHAPTER SEVEN

The last remaining month of the summer passed quickly. Before I knew it, I was out with Derek shopping for school supplies and finding great clothing deals for my own wardrobe on the summer clearance racks. The thought of putting on anything heavier than a g-string seemed hideous at the time because the weather was still excessively hot. We had little spurts of rainfall at the end of August, officially ending the drought. It really wasn't much rain to get that excited over. Then came Hurricane Floyd.

I made it into work that Monday morning in September before heaven's floodgates burst open. Sue Adelsberg cancelled her appointment due to illness, so I used the extra time I had to go over Mick Dillon's file. In the weeks I'd been analyzing him, I had learned much about his strengths and weaknesses regarding love. On the positive side, Mick had an openness and passion for love itself. His ability to surrender to love - a stage that many people, especially men, had difficulty getting passed – would most likely be easy for him. On the down side, he seemed to have a desperate need in him to fall in love and I needed to know exactly what that need was. My guess, compiled from talks I'd had with him, was because Mick needed a certain identity that he felt love could bring him.

One thing that I did know for certain was that Mickey Dillon was a lost soul. I was just hoping that he was ready to be found. He may have had the eyes of a child, but inside, I could tell he hurt like a man.

He came through my door with his hair dripping wet and his pale green shirt stuck to his firm body. I could smell the musky scent of his cologne from behind my desk. He looked incredibly sexy.

He laughed. "I'm so sorry I'm dripping all over the place. It's really starting to come down out there."

"Good, I'm glad," I responded as I handed him a roll of paper towels that I kept in one of my desk drawers. "My poor grass is so burnt. We could use a good drenching."

Mick passed a light smile my way and continued his task of drying off before sitting down.

"Mick, I would like to start off this session with a discussion about certain obstacles that may prevent you from experiencing the emotion of being in love. And a main obstacle that usually needs to be addressed is fear."

"Are you suggesting that I'm afraid to fall in love?" he asked. "If that was the case, then why would I be looking for it?"

"No, I'm not saying that," I replied. "But love and fear very often touch, and people like you, who have gone through some difficult things, sometimes carry fear around as a kind of familiar emotion. And I'm not just speaking about fear itself, but of self-doubt, confusion, despair, hopelessness, most of the common human frailties."

He looked concerned. "Do you think I'm frail?"

"No, but I do see a tremendous amount of vulnerability in you."

Mick flinched. I could tell he didn't like the word vulnerable. "Well, I have weaknesses like everyone else. Why would you say I'm any more vulnerable than anyone else?"

"Do you think you're lovable?" I asked Mick.

"What? What kind of question is that?"

I felt bad for the position I put Mick in, for I knew I had just embarrassed him. But I hadn't been voted best marriage therapist of the year by just pussyfooting around.

"Are you offended by that question, Mick? Why? Is it embarrassing to feel lovable? Discomfort arose in you because love can feel too personal, even for yourself. It pokes into those compartments where our negative self-image is stored. Falling in love means going there. That's what love demands. True love is more dangerous than most people are willing to admit. It arouses the same discomfort as dreams where you find yourself totally naked in public. To love another person involves opening up your whole being. Do you think you are able to do that, Mick?"

He remained silent and I could tell I hit a nerve.

"Mick, what I'm getting at is that it would be very hard to share your soul with another if you're not able to be in touch with it yourself."

The same awkward shyness that Mick exhibited in his first visit with me had appeared again. He looked nervous, uncomfortable, and unable to connect his eyes with mine. "Do you mind if I take a quick smoke break?"

"Already? Out in this rain?"

He looked disappointed. "Oh, I forgot."

He then paired his green eyes with mine and I could see an aching need in him. He really looked as though he needed pacifying.

I gave in. "Okay, you can have your smoke in here. Just go over by the window and crack it a bit. And please try to keep your ashes off the floor." I handed him my empty coffee cup.

He quietly walked over to the window and lit up a cigarette. "Have you ever smoked before, Dr. Simmons?"

"No."

"Why not?"

I shrugged. "Can't say that the idea ever appealed to me."

"Why don't you come over here and try it?" he asked softly.

I was taken aback. "Oh, no. I'm not interested in that. Smoking is bad for your health and it smells gross, besides."

"Smoking a cigarette is not done for the sake of trying to harm yourself or to even make you smell bad. There's a certain pleasurable aspect to smoking a cigarette that I feel you'd enjoy."

"Like what?"

"Come over here and I'll show you."

I couldn't believe that my feet were obeying his wishes. I felt that was totally unprofessional on my part, but I did have my hand in analyzing this guy. I stood beside Mick at the window, listening to the sound of pouring rain, and I immediately started to drown in his compellingly persuasive voice.

"Now the appeal in a cigarette, for me, is the sensuality in it. You see, Dr. Simmons, a cigarette to me is a lot like love. It's sucking in that smoke into the very core of you, and then releasing it back into the world."

Mick took a slow, generous draw of his cigarette, held onto the smoke for a moment, and then released it gracefully through his full lips into the air. "Why don't you have a try, Dr. Simmons?"

"No, no thank you."

"Why not? Are you afraid of a little smoke? Are you afraid to open yourself up to the pleasurable possibilities it can offer you?"

I didn't know what he was trying to get at with his subtle irony. But it was highly inappropriate. I walked back to my desk.

"Very interesting analogy you had there with the cigarette, Mick," I stated as he retook his seat. "Any other good ones you know that you'd like to tell me about?"

He gave a quick smile, and spoke with the fragility I had denounced on him earlier. "If you think my analogy on love was good, then you should hear the one I have on life. Life to me is like playing a game of cards. Sometimes, you're dealt a shitty hand in life. So, your best option would be to take a gamble. Sometimes you win, sometimes you lose. You'll always find yourself trying to get that Ace. The Ace represents different things to different people, but in the end it's all about power. You don't want anybody else controlling the cards in your life. You want to be the one in control of the game. To be the dealer. To be the cardholder. Do you know who's holding the cards in your life right now, Dr. Simmons? Is it you? Is it God? Or, could it be someone else?"

"Who are you?" I asked wryly. "Why did you come here?"

Mick looked confused. "What do you mean, Dr. Simmons?"

"Mr. Dillon, you claim you are here to seek out my help for yourself, yet, you seem to enjoy probing into certain aspects of my life. Remember, we are here to talk about you. Not me. I'm the doctor.

60

You're the patient."

He apologized. "Excuse me, I didn't mean to probe into your life. For my part, I was just having conversation with you. I'm new at this therapy stuff, so I guess I should remind myself that the conversation is supposed to be one-sided."

After delivering the final words to his apology, he proceeded to gaze at me with a hypnotic stare. I began to wonder exactly what it was that Mickey Dillon was searching for. Was it love he longed for? Or was it just desire? For, love and desire are essentially different.

The best way to distinguish the basis of the two can easily be determined from the way a person has sex. Working with couples, it was easy to find out a person's sexual habits just by asking their mate. In Mickey Dillon's case, I lacked a sexual mate to speak to.

That's when I thought of Annie.

CHAPTER EIGHT

"**A**re you *crazy*?" she asked, while wiping the spilled cola from my counter top.

I knew Annie would think I was going a bit overboard with the favor I asked of her. But I thought it was quite clever, at the time.

"Isn't something like that illegal?"

"No one else has to know about it, Annie. I want this to stay strictly between us. You have to swear to me you won't tell another living soul about this. It would look really bad for my profession."

She walked her way over to my side, picking up a towel to help dry the dinner plates I was washing. "You really want me to do this?"

I was a little surprised by Annie's apprehensiveness to partake in my scheme. She loved a good challenge, especially when it came to men. All I asked her to do was to head out Friday evening and engage in a little flirtatious conversation with the bartender, Mick Dillon, while secretly recording it for me.

"Yeah, it would mean a lot to me, Annie."

"I don't get it, Mags. Why do you want to do something like this?"

"I can't get into too much personal detail with you, Sis. I'm just trying to help this man out with a little problem he's having and I need to get a better handle on how he interacts with his prospective women."

"Hey! Are you talking about that guy you mentioned to me before, the one who wants to learn about falling in love?"

I frowned at her realization. "Yeah, but please don't ask me for details."

"And what makes you think he'd have an interest in flirting with me?"

I looked at her dryly. She smiled at my implied message.

"So, all I have to do is hide this little recording device in my purse, plop it on the counter, and flirt with this guy while it's recording."

"Yep."

"Okay, that sounds easy enough."

"Oh, and one more thing," I said finishing up my final dish. "If he wants to sleep with you, do it. And take some mental notes on the act for me too."

Annie's eyes blew up like a balloon being filled with helium. "Now you want me to *sleep* with the guy? I can't believe it! Who do you think you are? My pimp or something?"

"Just make sure you use a condom, darling. This guy may have been around the park a couple of times, and God only knows what kind of horses he's been riding on."

Skepticism filled the pores of her porcelain skin. "First of all, what makes you think that I'd want to sleep with this guy? I might think he's a dog or something, ya know."

"Don't worry, I can assure you, you definitely will find him attractive. I just have one more thing to tell you about that is very important," I spoke with a stern tone while looking into Annie's jade eyes. "Whatever you do, do not fall for this man. And he can't ever know that we are sisters, understand?"

"Wow," Annie said, her breath caught in her throat. "I feel like I'm being part of a secret spy mission. Don't you think you are taking things a bit too far for the sake of your job?"

Before I could answer Annie, Derek ran in the kitchen, asking me if I was ready to take him to his soccer game.

"Sweetie, Aunt Annie is gonna take you to your game this evening so I can keep my appointment to get my hair done. Is that okay?"

"Kewl!" he answered with excitement. "I like it when Aunt Annie takes me to my school stuff. My friends think she's really hot."

I laughed. "You see, Annie? Even the prepubescent boys love you"

She smirked. "Hip, hip hooray. I got a bunch of twelve-year-olds who've got a crush on me. What an amazing feat. I'm so lucky."

"Don't worry, Aunt Annie," consoled Derek. "Not all the guys are twelve. Most of them are thirteen already. And I'm gonna be thirteen in a few weeks."

She rolled her eyes at me while she made her way towards the door. "Oh, Derek, honey. That makes me feel so much better."

"Good luck on Friday!" I shouted out to her. "Call me first thing Saturday morning!!"

Greg and I were able to sneak in a quickie Saturday morning before heading out to Derek's soccer game. My body was thrilled that it was getting a lay, but my mind was too preoccupied to allow my flesh to delight in what was happening. Greg sensed my distraction.

"What's on your mind, Mag? You seem a little on edge this morning."

"Oh, nothing much," I murmured, while rubbing my face into my husband's chest hair. "I'm just waiting for a phone call from Annie. I told her to call me early this morning. I hope she calls before Derek's game, that's all."

Greg stroked my hair. "Is everything okay?"

"Yeah, just girl stuff," I answered him.

"Good. You know, if you ever need me for anything, Mag, I'm here. Just ask me, okay?"

After two calls to her apartment and one to her cell phone, I'd just about given up that I'd hear from Annie before my son's game. It was 11:30, and we had to get going. Curiosity burned a deep hole in my mind, so I told Annie to call me on my cell phone when she received my messages.

It was unusually windy on that Saturday so I took a light jacket with me. By the time we arrived on the field, many of the seats were taken. I kissed Derek and wished him luck, while Greg headed over to what were probably the last two vacancies I could spot in the bleachers. It only took me a few seconds to figure out why that particular spot had remained open.

"Hi Maggie! Hi Greg! How are you two doing?"

Greg passed me a look of disgust, leaned in and whispered into my ear. "Nice goin', Mag. Of all the spots you could've picked at this field, you go and pick a seat by Jill Coopersmith."

I returned his look back to him.

"We're doing good, Jill, thanks."

"Oh good. I guess Derek is playing today, huh?"

No, Jill. We are just here for the hell of it, I thought. "Yeah, Derek's playing today. I guess your Dougie is here today to play as well."

"Yeah, my little Dougie. He scored three points for the team in Wednesday's game. Gosh, they grow up so fast, don't they?"

"Well," Greg interrupted. "If you ladies don't mind, I'm gonna head down to the sidelines and have a little game strategy talk with Coach Grimes. I'll be back later."

I couldn't believe that Greg was leaving me alone with Jill. Then again, I could not blame him.

Jill continued. "Oh, I didn't know your husband was friendly with Coach Grimes."

"Well, he isn't too much," I explained. "But Greg is starting to show some interest in becoming a substitute coach in case the boys need one."

"That's wonderful, Maggie. Has he ever done any coaching before?"

"No, not really. But Greg seems to be taking a more of an interest in Derek's activities lately. He's always been close to Derek and all, but I think they've grown a lot closer lately. I don't know. Maybe all this is Greg's way of making it up to Derek for having to work so much these past several months."

"Maybe it's Derek's age now," Jill responded.

I hadn't given that much thought. "You think so?"

"Absolutely. I see some of that too in how my husband is now with

Doug. Our sons are at the age now where they're not just kids anymore. They are becoming young men. They really need and look up to their fathers at this stage in their lives. Sometimes, you may notice that they might distance themselves from us, their mothers, in odd about ways."

"Yes," I said with a laugh. "Derek hates it now if I kiss or hug him in public."

Jill nodded in agreement. "Yes, because they associate that with feminine things and they want to be men now! Have you guys had the sex talk with your son yet?"

"You mean about the birds and the bees? We had that a few years ago. Derek knows where babies come from. And they showed the kids a film last year in sixth grade about their bodies and the changes it will go through."

"No, that's not the sex talk I'm referring to. I'm talking about the one about how to use protection. Ya know, how to use a condom."

I was outraged. "No, I haven't talked to him about that stuff yet! He's still too young to be sexually active. He's got a few more years to go before he starts any screwing around."

Jill shook her head. "Oh, no, Maggie. You'd better get your son prepared for that kind of thing now. You wouldn't believe the things that my Dougie tells me. He says there is this new game going around school called the goodnight kiss where these girls will perform fellatio on a boy in a dark movie theater. And then I heard from Holly Mathers that she overheard her twelve-year-old on the phone one night talking with another girl about different boys' penis size."

I was stunned.

"I already had the talk with Doug and gave him a pack of condoms, just in case. I'm not ready to become a grandparent yet. And it's important to keep the communication lines open with your kid. I'm sure my Dougie will never feel uncomfortable telling me anything."

I looked out in the distance for my son as the players ran on the field at the start of the game. I couldn't imagine him, at such a tender age, experimenting with sex yet. And I, unlike Jill Coopersmith, was not even going to encourage him to even think about it.

After a victorious game, many of the kids on Derek's team were celebrating by heading out to Friendly's for some ice-cream. Greg offered to drive some of the kids and then take them home afterward. I was anxious to get home myself, so I bummed a ride off Jill.

When I arrived home, I ran to my phone to find a message blinking on my answering machine. I pressed firmly on the play button.

BEEP. "Hey Mags, it's Annie. I got your messages. I was gonna call your cell phone, but forgot your new number and you didn't leave it for me...so... I'll be home a few minutes for now and I'll probably be out the rest of the day. And night. So, I guess I'll call you tomorrow. Bye!" *BEEP.*

Oh, I was irate. The suspense of what may have happened the night before between Annie and Mick was killing me. I dialed Annie's number and got her machine. I dialed Annie's cell phone and got her voicemail. I was just about out the door to hop in my car and drive over Annie's when I suddenly realized how paradoxical I was behaving. I laughed at myself.

The next day, Annie finally called in the early afternoon. I grabbed the cordless phone and headed outside to the deck in my backyard for privacy.

"Well, Annie, don't keep me in suspense any longer. How did you make out at the hotel the other night?"

There was a long pause.

"Oh, very well. I think," she finally spoke.

"So, you met him, right?"

"Yeah."

"And you got talking with him?"

"Yeah."

"And was your conversation on the flirtatious side?"

"Oh, you could definitely say that."

"Great! Did the recorder work okay?"

"Oh yeah, I think it worked fine."

"Wonderful! I'll hop in my car now and head over to pick it up. I owe you one, Annie."

"Ummm, I don't think it's a good idea that you come over right now, Mags."

I was befuddled. "Why not?"

"Because Mick is asleep in my bed right now."

"*What*? What is he doing there? Why is he at your place right now?"

"Oh, Mags," Annie sighed, "I think I've met my soul mate."

CHAPTER NINE

Sue and Harry bickered ferociously while I mentally recalled the short, vague conversation I shared with my sister the previous day. She told me that since she was unable to speak with Mick at her place, she would call me again last night after he'd left. She never called. I was left without any details of what had happened between them.

"...and what's your professional opinion on this issue, Dr. Simmons?"

Harry's voice suddenly called me back to earth, to be the mediator for Peg and Al Bundy.

"Well, my opinion is that...," I said, quickly glancing at my watch, "being that we're out of time for this week's session, I'll think the issue through a little deeper and discuss it with you next week. Okay?"

I couldn't believe it! I'd been practicing my counseling for nearly ten years and not once, until that very moment, had I let my mind wander so far that I was oblivious to what my patients were discussing with me. That caught me off guard and frightened me a bit.

Mick arrived for his appointment looking a little more tired than usual. He had always appeared in a relaxed state, but today he showed signs of exhaustion by the way he held and moved his body. Either that, or he could have been drunk.

"Hello, Mick. How was your weekend?"

"Just great, Dr. Simmons," he spoke slowly, dropping onto the chair. "And yours?"

"It was nice, thank you. Glad to hear yours went pretty well," I replied, while dying to know what had happened between him and my sister. But, of course, I had to play it cool. Unfortunately, the basis for the particular session I planned to have with Mick today was going to be based on the material Annie was supposed to have recorded for me. I did not yet know the content of their conversation, so I was just going to improvise.

"Mick, before I start my session with you this morning, I was wondering if there was anything on your mind that you'd like to talk about. Or, if maybe there were any questions that you needed to ask me."

Mick shook his head.

I smiled. "Great! In that case, why don't we go ahead and..."

"Wait!" he shouted, surprising himself. "There is a little something I was wondering about that I'd like to ask you, if you don't mind."

"Please, go right ahead."

Mick leaned forward, resting his elbows on his knees. "Dr. Simmons, do you believe in love at first sight?"

"No, Mick, I don't," I responded. "I believe there are romantic, spiritual steps a person must go through before they can possibly get to the final stage of true love."

"So, you don't think it's possible for two people to meet, be able to skip all the bullshit steps, and just naturally be meant for each other and instantly be in love."

"Professionally speaking, no, I really don't think that is possible. I believe you can find yourself infatuated with another person in a short period of time, but to reach that true level of love, you can't get to it by leaping over those other important steps. That's like preparing a recipe, say for a cake, and leaving out vital ingredients. Your cake may appear okay when you take it out of the oven, but give it a little time and you'll find it will just crumble to pieces."

Mick nodded his head, understanding what I had meant. "Steps. I have to take steps. What steps are there?"

"Well, rather than call them steps, let's call them phases. The first phase a person goes through would be the initial phase of attraction, of course. Attraction starts when a person singles out another person, for

70

reasons usually unknown and subconscious, because they are smitten by them. Sometimes it can be a simple thing, like a person's smile, the way they wear their hair, the scent of their cologne or perfume that sparks an initial attraction for somebody. Next, comes the infatuation stage, which some may confuse with love..."

Mick let out a soft, playful grunt.

I continued. "And in that stage, a person's beloved becomes all desirable and all enveloping. In the depths of infatuation, the lover's fantasy life can become both wild and extreme. If there are no insurmountable barriers, the phase of courtship will begin next. The beloved is wooed in order to create the same attraction the lover so overwhelmingly feels."

"Wow," Mick said, grinning. "I really didn't realize how complicated all this love stuff is."

"You know what's funny? It's really the opposite that is true. Love is truly simple. It's usually the rest of the stuff in our lives that makes it appear so complicated."

He passed me an endearing look.

"Anyhow, if the courtship is successful, intimacy follows. Through intimacy, the union of two people begins to be played out in the real world rather than within an isolated psyche. Reality is revealed as they test the waters of unmasking fantasy. Once fantasy is unmasked, the lovers will either find themselves fallen back to earth, or they will have learned from their experience and be ready to integrate it into love's further growth. Although it happens spontaneously, falling in love isn't accidental. It is a choice."

Mick appeared confused. "I don't get it. How is it a choice and all? Have you ever met someone in your life, and in the instant you first laid eyes on him, you've felt that you were destined for something?"

Ha, if he only knew. "Yes. Speaking on the basis of intuition."

"No, Dr. Simmons. I'm talking more than simple intuition here. I'm talking about meeting someone, and in the very instant that you lay eyes on each other, you are totally captivated by one another. Like your paths were undeniably fated to cross and you feel this, like,

71

intense spiritual bond. You can't tell me that it would be a choice for someone to feel that way. It just happens. Do you know what I'm talking about?"

I found myself smiling with the thrill of anticipation welling up inside me. "Why do you ask such a question, Mick?"

He sank deeper into his chair. "Because, I think I met someone. Someone that I think I could fall in love with. Someone I think I could be in love with already."

"Really? Tell me about her."

His eyes went passive. "Well, I'm not ready to discuss her too much with you right now, Dr. Simmons. My main concern here is that I get this falling in love thing right, and don't screw anything up. The woman, I'll refer to her as Jane, is one of the most amazing women I've met in my life."

Jane? Why did he have to refer this woman as Jane? It made me feel as though he didn't quite trust me. Or trust enough in himself to be totally free with me. I wondered, and assumed, that this Jane he was speaking of was Annie. And if it was Annie, I was in big trouble.

Mick spoke highly of his Jane, saying he had never felt so emotionally drawn and moved by a woman before. He talked of her beauty, charm, wit, and sensuality. He recalled "feeling a power greater than himself standing before him," and was fully entranced when they had first greeted each other. He didn't know if Jane felt the same intensity of emotions upon their first meeting as he did, and expressed a strong desire to me that he wished to handle the situation appropriately.

"And what of Alexis in all of this?" I asked.

"Alex is cool," he answered. "I'm not going to tell her about any of this until... until I see how all this unfolds. There is no point of her knowing anything now."

"Does Alexis know that you are seeking therapy?"

Mick scratched the underneath of his chin. "No."

"So, she is unaware that you come and see me Monday mornings?"

"Yep. She doesn't know anything about this."

I knew Mick was lying, but I didn't know the reason why. "Then, where does she think you might be right now, or those other past Monday mornings that you've been here?"

"Out taking a walk," he replied. "That is always a good excuse to give someone when you have to sneak out and do something. That, and I've told Alex that sometimes, after working Sunday night, I crash at my buddy's apartment that is close to the hotel, when I'm too tired or too drunk to drive. And that, actually, is true."

"Do you think it's possible that Alexis may harbor any feelings for you?"

Mick looked uncomfortable with the question asked of him, but answered abruptly. "I don't know exactly what Alex's feelings are for me. I've never asked her, nor do I ever intend to. What we have between us is nice and okay. There is no need to fuck that up with feelings."

"But, you are willing to venture into having feelings for this Jane girl. What makes the difference for you?"

Mick delivered me a come hither stare. "You know what, Dr. Simmons? That's a good question. I think you should stop by at the M.P. Lounge this Friday evening so you can meet Jane yourself. Maybe you could tell me the reason."

"Oh no, Mick, I couldn't possibly do that," I replied with a gentle laugh. "I don't make a practice of socializing with my patients outside of my office."

"C'mon. We don't have to have a patient-doctor relationship that evening. We could act like neighbors that night instead."

I shook my head. "No, I'm sorry. I can't do that."

Mick slowly rose from his chair and pulled out a pack of cigarettes from his shirt pocket. He motioned that he was interested in taking a smoke break and walked towards the door.

Before he exited the room, he turned to me with a devilish grin on his face, "Oh, by the way Dr. Simmons, just so you know, the name of the girl you're gonna meet on Friday night isn't really Jane. It's Annie."

KELLY O'CALLAN

I was hoping for a miracle that evening which would make Annie arrive to our yoga session early so we could do some important chatting beforehand.

I didn't get the miracle.

I don't know which one of us was more frustrated at the inability to communicate during the workout. I had so much to say and ask as did Annie. But, being as vain as we are, neither one of us was willing to skip class for the sake of satisfying our need for each other's ear-chewing.

After an intense session with Paula, Annie and I walked to the coffeehouse next door, where we anxiously tried to pull information about Mick from one another. Both of us were apparently eager to listen, but not talk.

"C'mon, Maggie! I know Mick must've said something about me today. He spent the entire weekend with me. Please don't keep me in the dark."

I took a sip of my de-caffeinated French roast, practically burning my tongue off in the process. I grimaced from the sensation. "Annie, you know I can't tell you anything about my sessions with Mick. It's a patient-doctor confidentiality thing."

"Yeah, but I'm your sister," she pleaded.

"It doesn't matter who you are. Don't take it personally, Annie, but for me to disclose any of the private conversation I had with Mick would be totally unprofessional."

"Yeah, as if asking me to secretly record the guy isn't unprofessional," she remarked.

"Hey, I never told you anything about the man," I snapped. "And where are those tapes anyway?"

Annie grinned, her smirk conveying mischief. "Actually, you already did tell me something about Mick, Ms. Unprofessional. You told me he came to you because he wanted to learn how to fall in love. And who knows? The answer to his problem might be right here on this tape."

74

She gently pulled the small recorder out of her purse and placed it on the table, never letting go. As I reached for it, she pulled it away, shoving it back into her bag.

"No, no, no," she cackled. "What makes you think I'm gonna hand these tapes over to you? That would be an unprofessional thing, now wouldn't it?"

"Okay, Annie. I get your point. Quit your fooling around and just give me the tape."

"And what do I get in return?" she asked, sly as a thief.

"C'mon Annie, stop acting like a baby."

"Oh, I'm not acting like a baby at all. What do I get for this tape?"

"Are you trying to get money out of me?"

"No," she responded with a chuckle.

I was frustrated with her. "Then what the hell exactly is it that you want from me, Annie?"

She leaned in closer to me and whispered. "I spy for you, and in return, you spy for me."

"*What?*" I asked in alarm.

"It's simple," she spoke with a reassuring smile. "I keep recording my conversations with Mick and hand them over to you. You keep analyzing Mick and keep me informed on his weekly sessions. And bam! You are successful at making him able to fall in love... with me."

"*Are you nuts?*" I yelled in a whisper. "Annie, I don't ever want you to see this guy again!"

"What? Mags, how can you say that to me? He's my soul mate!"

I was manic. "Christ, Annie! Get a grip. You only met the guy a couple of days ago! This is nuts. The whole idea of mine was nuts and wrong and I'm sorry now that I ever came up with that stinkin' ploy! Just forget this all happened. Just forget that you've ever met Mickey Dillon."

Annie rose from her seat. "I can't do that, Maggie. And you can't stop me from seeing him either!"

On the drive home that evening, the possible consequences that could have been created by my wrong doing became a little clearer to me. I would have never guessed that my piddling expedient could cause such a ruckus. I thought things couldn't possibly get any worse for me that night. I was wrong.

"Hey, Honey. How was your day?" Greg asked from behind his widely spread newspaper.

I groaned. "Don't ask."

I heard the sudden crinkling of newspaper as he folded it upon his lap. "Oh, Mag, it sounds like you had a shitty day."

I hung up my jacket and dropped heavily onto the couch, across from Greg in his chair.

"Don't worry, Mag. I have something for you to look forward to."

"Did we win the lottery?"

"No. But I ran into that new neighbor of ours after work. You know, that guy I was playing volleyball with at the block party. The one that lives with that Alexis LeNoir woman."

I felt my eyes bulge. "You mean Mickey Dillon?"

"Yeah, that's the guy. How'd you know his name? Anyway, he works at the Mason Pierce Hotel tending bar in the lounge and invited us to go there on Friday night. He said they'll be having karaoke there that night and they get a great crowd in. I told him it sounded like fun and that we'd go. How about it?"

"No, Greg. I don't want to go."

"Why not?"

"I don't think it's such a great idea."

"Why not? We haven't gone out on a Friday night like that in awhile."

"Well, I can't go. I have other plans that night."

"Okay. Then I'll go myself."

"No! You can't!" I shrieked.

Greg's face contorted. "What? What the hell's your problem, Maggie?"

"I need you to be home that night for Derek. I don't trust him home alone on a Friday night," I lied.

"Taken care of. Derek's gonna sleep over my sister Carol's house Friday night. He's all excited about it because he hasn't been able to spend much time with his cousins since school started."

I was trapped. Cornered. If Greg went to the M.P. Lounge and saw Annie there with Mick, I was screwed. And if Greg didn't go this week, it didn't mean he wouldn't show up another time, since the idea was now planted in his head. I could have strangled that Mick. I didn't know what he was up to. Why did he have to involve my husband in his obvious ploy to get me to the M.P. Lounge on Friday evening? Did he have a particular agenda planned for me? As, in all honesty, I had for him?

To keep things from going from bad to worse, my only solution was to tell my husband about what was going on, and what I had done.

"Maggie! *Have you lost your mind?* I can't *believe* you would do such a thing!"

"I know," I countered. "I know I made a mistake."

"A mistake? A *mistake* is what you're calling it? It's down right ludicrous!"

I expected my husband to act sourly about my unprofessional manipulation, but, I never imagined he would react so enraged.

"What the hell were you thinking, Maggie? What would make you do such a thing? Why would you do such a thing?"

"I don't know."

"What? You must have had a reason!"

I hated being drilled. "I don't know... I guess I just wanted to be able to do the best job I could for the guy and in order to do that, there were certain things I had to know about him."

"So, you get your sister to perform an illegal activity to help you out? And in the process, you breech your doctor/patient confidentiality with the guy. I can't believe it. That's not like you!"

Frustration billowed up inside me. "Nobody ever said I was perfect! And who are you to speak? You can't tell me that you've never crossed the line in an attempt to persuade some of your big money clients to sign on with your company!"

"Hey, this is not about me."

We sat for a moment in silence.

"I don't know what to do," I finally mumbled.

"You gotta fix this," Greg said, as he came over to sit beside me.

I looked at him. "How?"

"We go to the hotel on Friday night. When we spot Annie there, we'll look totally surprised to see her there. And she should look surprised to see us there as well. Everything will look totally coincidental. Call your sister up and put her wise to it. And by the way, how did this Mick guy end up going to you for counseling anyhow?"

I frowned. "A recommendation... by Jill Coopersmith."

CHAPTER TEN

I sat nervously in the BMW, chewing my bottom lip, as I tried to prepare myself for the act I'd have to perform when we arrived at the hotel. I called my sister a few days earlier to let her know that Greg and I would be there that evening, and for her to act surprised in front of Mick, when we'd run into each other. We would just laugh at the coincidence that we knew each other and were, in fact, sisters. It seemed like a simple plan.

But, Annie wasn't going for it. In fact, she strongly opposed the idea. She wanted to keep the fact that she and I were sisters a complete secret from Mick. She felt that if he knew of our relationship, he'd quickly decide to stop seeing her. I understood Annie's dilemma and consoled her about it, but insisted we not play games anymore and resolve this issue by eliminating any further fallacies. Unfortunately for me, Annie would not budge. She was quite adamant on how she felt about the issue. So adamant, in fact, that she threatened to tell Mick of my dishonorable infraction if I would not abide by her wishes. I couldn't believe I was being blackmailed by my own sister. She was undeniably in a state of heightened infatuation with this guy. There probably wasn't a thing I could do about it. That didn't mean I was happy that my sister was blindly absorbed by a gigolo with a gambling addiction. It meant, that for the time being, I had to go along with her wishes.

Earlier that evening, I told Greg there was no point for us to go to the M.P. Lounge since Annie still wanted to keep our secret extant. He laughed my suggestion off, noting that he didn't care. He wanted to go out and have a good time anyway. But I personally felt he was getting a cheap thrill out of seeing me tortured by this situation. He was like that sometimes.

As we entered the A1 hotel, I reminded Greg on how to react when we were introduced to Annie.

"I can't believe she wants us to act like we've never met her before. Is she out of her mind?"

"Yes, she is," I responded. "That's what happens when you've gone head-over-heels over someone."

"It makes no sense," Greg said with a grunt, as a bellhop pointed out to us the direction to the lounge. "If she likes the guy that much, how does she think she's going to handle it when it gets to the point that he'll want to meet her family one day? How will she ever be able to explain 'meeting us' here, then?"

"I don't know," I responded, aggravated. "I guess that will be something we'll just have to figure out later."

Greg rolled his eyes as he opened the lounge door for me. "God, you women are just plain crazy. I swear it."

The lounge was quite large inside with an oval bar in the center of the room. The furniture was made of dark oak and the decor consisted of simple, black-and-white photos of local celebrities along the wall with soft, gold lights illuminating them. There was a crowd of roughly thirty people there when we first arrived, which gradually increased by the hour. The smoke was thick and the music was loud; which I found to be quite distasteful for such a well-established hotel. Nonetheless, the patrons seemed to be enjoying themselves.

I grabbed two chairs for Greg and me at one end of the bar. I quickly spotted Mick on the other side of the room chatting with a young redhead. It felt strange to me to see him out of the context of my office. Even in a room filled with many people, he still conveyed a strong presence about himself. I scanned the room speedily to search for Annie and came up empty.

A plain, yet pretty barmaid approached Greg and me as we nestled in our seats.

"Hi, my name is Sara and I'll be your server this evening. What can I get you both to drink?"

"A cosmopolitan, please," I answered.

"And I'll have a vodka martini, no olive," Greg said.

When I gazed at the entrance area, after placing my drink order, I spotted Annie. She looked stunning, as usual, and winked knowingly at me. My eyes then focused on Mick, who was lost in a deep gaze of his own, as he looked in Annie's direction. The two met up, hugged, then sat at a small vacant table and instantly engaged in conversation. As much as I didn't want to admit it, I thought they looked like a beautiful couple after seeing them together.

Within minutes, Mick popped behind the bar and headed in our direction. "Hey, you guys made it! Great to see you both. Anything I can get you to drink this evening?"

Just as he finished his words, the barmaid pushed her way past Mick, and I caught glimpse of a nasty look she directed at him.

"That's alright, I've already taken care of these two," Sara snapped at him, while placing our drinks on the counter. "But you can make yourself useful and help out some of the people on the other end, why don't you?"

As she turned and left our presence, Mick leaned in towards us. "Sorry about that, guys. Sara's okay. She just gets...you know...a little funny with me sometimes. I can't read her."

Greg chuckled. "I know what you mean, Mick. Sometimes these women just don't make any sense."

I frowned at that remark, and Mick saw it.

"Aw, c'mon, Greg. You have a lovely wife here," Mick said, pausing and looking keenly into my eyes. "Surely you can't say a negative word about her."

"I wouldn't dare," Greg remarked. "She'd find a way to get back at me one way or another for it."

Normally a comment like that from my husband would have pissed me off, but I was so lost in the beauty of Mick's searching gaze that I didn't give a rat's ass about what Greg said.

"I'll be back," stated Mick as he trotted over to the other end of the bar.

I was angst-ridden about the moment he would return to us, totally petrified about how natural or unnatural my reaction would appear when he'd bring Annie over to meet me. I tried to calm myself as the hours passed, sipping carefully on my cosmopolitan so to not make myself too drunk for when the moment of truth would come.

But, the moment never came. Mick kept himself busy with his bartending and occasionally got up to perform a couple of karaoke songs. He sat with Annie when he had a few free moments, but left her to sit alone while he worked.

When Greg and I were ready to leave for the night, we waived our goodbyes to Mick and he thanked us for coming and encouraged us to come by again. Greg told him we would. We left the M.P. Lounge that evening never having spoken a word to Annie at all. I was a little shocked to find that what should have been a relief to me, actually felt more like a disappointment.

When Mick met with me on that following Monday for our hourly session, he had not mentioned any of the specifics of his 'Jane' or 'Annie' to me, which I had found quite odd. I did end up asking Mick if this Annie woman had shown up at the M.P. Lounge the Friday evening I was there, since he had surely expressed a strong interest that I meet her. He surprised me when he answered with a 'no'. I didn't understand the change in his attitude about Annie, at least, not from my side of the desk.

Things, according to Annie, were going quite well for her and Mick. In the weeks that passed, they began seeing, or at least talking to each other, on a daily basis. On the weekends, they were inseparable. Annie never gave me any specifics of their relationship together, and I was glad for it. Yet, I had to admit, my curiosity level burned high. I had never seen my sister happier than she had recently become, and I was going to do everything I could possibly do to ensure that happiness for her. I even offered to skip Trista's wedding, which I truthfully wasn't looking forward to attending in the first place, so Annie could take Mick. That way, I could still keep our relationship a secret for her. I stressed to Annie that, at some point, we would have to reveal to Mick that we actually knew, and were related to each other. Annie expressed she wanted a little time to connect with Mick on a deeper level before revealing our relationship. In the meantime, we would have to come up with a strategy that could safely evince our dirty little secret.

But, in the end, we never had to figure out that strategy. For, it was the events of a tragedy that eventually forced us to unleash our truths.

CHAPTER ELEVEN

My heart leaped into my throat, as I stumbled out of bed, to frantically answer the ringing telephone on that Friday morning in mid-October. My eyes focused obscurely on a clock which read 5:38 a.m. A phone call that time of day was usually never a good one.

I followed the sound of the incessant, unnerving ringing which led me to a table in the living room, where the cordless phone lay. My first feeling, when seeing the phone there, was one of irritation because my son repeatedly forgot to hang the phone up to recharge overnight. I shook off that thought and grabbed the phone with anticipatory fear that something must be wrong.

"Hello?"

"Oh Mags, thank God you answered! I'm so sorry for calling you so early in the morning, but I need your help!"

Annie's voice sounded panicked.

"Annie? What the hell is going on?"

"Oh, you're not going to believe what happened. It's Alexis. She's dead."

"What? What happened?"

"I don't know," Annie cried, "But they have Mick and they're interrogating him right now. I'm down at the police station with him. You have to come down here now and tell these cops that you are his shrink, and that you know that Mick could never kill a person."

"Annie, hold on. I can't just barge in down there and say something like that."

"What are you saying, Mags? Don't you want to help me? Don't you want to help Mick?"

"Okay, Annie, calm down and stay put. I'm on my way there."

I placed the phone back onto the charger and made my way back up the stairs to my bedroom. To my surprise, Derek was sitting at the top of the steps, apparently eavesdropping on my conversation.

"Who was that on the phone, Mom?"

"It was Aunt Annie, honey."

"Is everything okay?"

"Yes. She's just having a problem right now that she needs me to help her with. I'm gonna get dressed and go out to help her and I don't know what time I'll be back. I'll leave a note for your father to make sure that you are up in time for school. So get back to bed."

Derek rose to his feet. "Hey, Mom?"

"What, sweetie?"

"I think something happened down the street. If you look out the window in my bedroom, you can see a bunch of flashing lights from cop cars. I think they're parked out front of that rich lady's house."

I tried to back my car out of the driveway as discreetly as I could. I noticed that many of my neighbors were standing outside their houses, and some were gathered closer to Alexis LeNoir's mansion. I decided to drive down the street in the opposite direction from where all the chaos was taking place. In a whim of curiosity, I peeped into my rear-view mirror where I could make out a policeman lifting up some yellow tape in order to allow an unwieldy gurney, draped in white sheets, to pass through. I became chilled with nausea.

The clock on my dashboard read 6:02 a.m. It was still dark and there was a slight cool dampness in the air. It was an eerie time of morning, and the sadness of the reality of an untimely death greatly affected me. I felt an overwhelming grief for Alexis LeNoir, even though I only met her once. She was, without a doubt, too young to die. But, what had happened to her? If she had been murdered, would Mick have been capable of doing so? And why? My intention when I reached the police station, was simply to provide emotional support to my sister. I was not going there to divulge my personal or professional beliefs about Mick Dillon to any law enforcement officer unless I was legally required to do so. I was hoping that Annie would understand that. But, after recalling her hysterics on the phone, I sincerely doubted she would be happy with me.

When I walked inside the station, Annie was not in sight. I went to the front desk and asked if an Annie Von Worth was there.

"She's the girl with the LeNoir case, right?"

"Yes."

"And who are you?"

"Her sister."

"Okay, M'aam. Ms. Von Worth is currently being questioned about the case, so you can have a seat in the waiting area there and she should be out shortly."

I took my seat in the waiting area. My heart raced. My palms were cold and sweaty. My limbs shook uncontrollably. I was scared. What exactly about, I couldn't say. Maybe I was scared for Annie. Maybe I was scared for Mick. Maybe I was scared about what happened to Alexis.

And maybe I was scared for myself. Undoubtedly, the secret Annie and I shared regarding Mick would surface. All a policeman had to do was ask Annie how she met Mick, and I'd be ruined. Just as that thought crossed my mind, my cell phone rang. I shoved my hand into my tiny, overstuffed purse and maneuvered it out.

"Hello?"

"Maggie, where are you?" Greg asked.

"I'm at the police station. Alexis LeNoir is dead. Annie called me to tell me that the police are interrogating Mick Dillon."

"Alexis LeNoir is dead? Oh God. So, please tell me why the hell you're down the police station. What does all this have to do with you?"

"Nothing," I answered. "I'm just here to help Annie out."

"Help Annie out with what? Does she have something to do with Alexis' death?"

"No, but I think the police may be asking her some questions about Mick now. I haven't seen her yet."

Greg spoke firmly. "Maggie, I want you to listen to me. Get your ass out of there now and come home."

"Why?"

"Just listen to me and trust me, Maggie. Get out of there now. You don't want to get involved with any of that crap. I know you are probably there with good intentions in mind, but believe me, once you show any type of involvement in this at all, the cops will remain all over you."

"Greg, I have nothing to hide. I didn't kill the woman! Why would the cops bother me?"

"Mag, would you just trust me!" Greg yelled. "Leave the station now! Don't dirty your name. Don't dirty our name."

"I can't leave yet. I told Annie that I'd come here to help her."

Greg let out a soft grunt. "Who are you really there to help out, Maggie? Do you think you're there to help Annie out? Or are you there to help out this Mick guy?"

I heard a door open and soft footsteps coming from a hallway. I looked up and saw my sister.

"Greg, I gotta go. I'll call you later," I said and flipped my phone switch to off.

I stood from my chair and Annie ran over to give me a hug. "Thanks for coming, Mags."

"Hey, is everything okay?"

Annie released herself from me, leaving her hands to rest on my arms. "Yeah, everything is gonna be okay now."

"Please, tell me what happened!"

I retook my seat and Annie grabbed the chair next to me.

"Well," she spoke softly, "Mick found Alexis dead in her bathtub when he got home a couple of hours ago. He called the cops and when they got to her house, they brought him down here. He called me before the cops arrived and told me about what happened to Alex. I told him I'd be right over. Just as I got there, the cops were shoving

Mick into a police car, so I ended up following them down here. And that's when I called you, a little after that. He was in the room so long, and I got a little nervous."

"And you wanted me to come down here to tell the cops what? That I don't think Mick's capable of murdering a person? I can't do that, Annie."

"That's okay, Mags. You won't have to," she spoke in a serious tone.

"What do you mean?"

"Mick will be okay now. He's got an alibi. I told the cops he was with me all night."

"You what? Annie, is that true?"

"Yes, it's true."

I thought for a moment. "Annie, if it's true that Mick was with you all night, then why would you ask me to come down here to give a character statement about Mick to the police, when you already knew he'd be in the clear?"

Annie had a dark sincerity brewing in her eyes. "Look, I don't care what you or anybody thinks. Mick and I were together all night. I refuse to let anyone or anything ever take him away from me!"

CHAPTER TWELVE

I sat in my office that Monday morning in a state of bewilderment. It was the same confusing state I had been in for the previous three days. I took several slow, deep breaths after the departure of the Adelsbergs, knowing which visitor would follow. This would be the first time I would see Mickey Dillon since Alexis' tragic death. I had read in the newspaper the day before that the reported cause of Alexis' death was by drowning. The manner of her death had been ruled accidental. Toxicology reports stated that there were large doses of anti-depressants found in Ms. LeNoir's blood, along with a high-level of alcohol consumption. It was concluded that Alexis had simply passed out while relaxing in her colossal-sized bathtub.

Slews of reporters and detectives had bombarded Birch Street in the days before the initial ruling on her death. I kept a low profile, staying indoors and ignoring the news reporter's knocks to my door. The LeNoir family had been prominent in our community for many decades, as participants in many popular fundraisers and big donors to local charitable events. The media repeatedly mentioned the great loss our town would experience with the passing of Alexis, the final member of the eccentric LeNoir dynasty.

Mick entered somberly into my office, his face etched in desperation.
"Hello, Mick. How are you holding up this morning?" I asked while struggling to control the quivering in my voice.

89

He was silent for a moment before he released his first words. When he spoke, his voice was edged with tension. "Not too good, Dr. Simmons. Not too good at all. I need some serious help."

He looked at me, his eyes transfixed in horror.

"Is there anything I'd be able to help you with?"

He sighed nervously. "No, nobody can help me."

"What's on your mind?"

Mick crossed his one leg over the opposite knee and shook his dangled foot heedlessly. "Nothing. I'm just really freaked out. Really freaked out about what happened to Alex."

I spoke unbiased and without emotion. "Yes, Mick, I understand how you must feel. It was a terrible thing that happened to her."

"I can't believe... I can't believe she's dead," he said, choking on his words.

"Yes, it was a horrible accident and..."

"It was no accident!" Mick's voice exploded as he rose from his chair. "I should have been there. I should have never left her alone the way I did that night. I should have known something like this would happen to her. It's my fault. Because of me, she's dead! She didn't deserve that."

Mick dropped back into his chair and covered the shame on his face with his hands. I began to hear the subtle sounds of sobbing that he was trying to hide.

I came out from behind my desk and pulled up a seat next to Mick. I put my hand on the back of his shoulder. "Mick, what happened to Alex was an accident. It was not your fault. Sometimes, horrible things like that just happen."

Mick dropped his hands from his face and composed his emotions. "You believe things like that just happen, Dr. Simmons?"

"Yes, there are some things in life that you just can't explain. And, I believe in God, and that He controls the major things that happen to us in our lifetime. Our purpose. Our fate. Mick, it was probably just Alexis' time to go. And, if God wanted her, He was going to take her. And there would've been nothing you could've done about that."

90

"I'm terrified of death. I'm totally scared of the unknown. Even all this crap about the millennium being the end of the world scares the shit out of me."

"Which may be the reason why you feel you need help with falling in love. Fear of the unknown. Make sense to you?"

"Yeah, I guess," he nodded. "By the way, Dr. Simmons, I wanted to let in on a little something I know."

"What's that?" I asked retaking my seat behind the desk.

Mick looked at me intently. "I know about Annie. I mean, that you two are sisters and all."

I froze, even though I assumed Annie had told him at the police station following Alexis' death. "How'd you find out?"

"Annie told me the other night. But, to tell you the truth, I actually knew it the night I met Annie. She had the same picture of your family in her wallet that you have on your desk. I figured you two may be related. I didn't want to freak either of you two out initially, which is why I asked you to go to the M.P. Lounge that Friday. So, that way, you could know about the situation. When you both kept quiet about knowing each other that evening, I felt maybe I should keep quiet about it, too. But, in thinking about the doctor-patient confidentiality thing, it's not like anything I tell to you would get back to Annie. So, there's nothing you or I or Annie should be concerned about. It was just a freak thing, right?"

"Right," I shrugged off.

"Just one of the things that happens, I guess. Like you say, God probably planned it that way. Annie and I were meant to meet. And probably you and I as well, don't you think Dr. Simmons?'

"Sure" I answered with an insipid smile.

Mick's face contorted from thought. "I'd like to see things your way, Dr. Simmons. You know, about you believing in God and fate and all. But, frankly, I don't. I believe that the God of purpose and fate may hold some of the cards of your hand in the game of life, but you hold some of your own cards as well. And if you don't keep on top of your hand, someone may come up and steal some of your cards, and play your hand their way. You should be careful and stop to pay attention to the hand you've been dealt in life, Dr. Simmons, because someone else may have their hand on your Ace. Just like someone else out there had control of Alexis'."

I spoke guardedly. "What are you trying to tell me, Mick? What is it about this card reference that you've brought up to me before?"

His eyes were worried, and I got the sense that he was trying to choose his words to me carefully.

"Nothing specific, Dr. Simmons. I'm just suggesting that it's a good idea to be aware of everything that's going on in your life. And not to be so naive as to think that you can't control the things that happen to you. You either win at life or you lose. Be smart enough to play the game for yourself. Be on top of things and know your strategy. And watch out for those you may be playing with."

"So, do you think Alexis played with the wrong people in the game of life? Is that why she lost?"

"Dr. Simmons, are you implying something about me?"

"Not at all," I responded. "I'm only trying to decipher what you are implying to me."

Mick's lips formed a crafty smile. "Alex was dealt some great cards in her life. Unfortunately, I don't think she knew how to hold her hand well. Great players can sense a thing like that, and manipulate an unfledged cardholder. Did I take advantage of Alex's good fortune? Sure I did. You and I both know I'd be lying if I said I didn't."

"Why do you believe someone 'stole her ace' as you put it? Did you take control of her hand, Mick? Was it you who took her ace?"

"No, I didn't exactly take her ace. But, I did steal her queen of hearts."

"Alright," I said feeling vexed. "Enough with this card talk. So, now that Alexis is gone, what will happen to Mickey Dillon? Where will you live now?"

"I'm going to look at an apartment when I leave here this morning, it's a few blocks down on Broad Street."

"An apartment here in town will cost you a small fortune. How will you afford something like that?"

"I'll be alright. It's just for a little while, anyway."

"A little while?"

Mick adjusted his seating. "Yeah, um... you know... until I find another place."

What I was interpreting him say was until he found another Alex.

"Have you been back to Alex's house since Friday morning?"

"The cops said I could go in and get my things after last night," he spoke sullenly. "I don't wanna go back in there. All I can picture is Alex lying dead there in her bathtub. I keep seeing it and it freaks me out. I'll never forget what she looked like. I've been having nightmares about it ever since."

"Perhaps, you may need a prescription for a tranquilizer. It might help you get some restful sleep until the trauma passes."

"I have prescriptions for Ambien. I've been taking something to help me sleep since I had my breakdown in '89. I'm lucky 'cause I have Annie there for me. She's going to meet me at the house after she's done with work so I don't have to go through it alone."

Annie definitely had to have a thing for this guy if she'd be willing to forgo her yoga class. She'd always been so anal about keeping herself fit.

"Mick, since we're on the subject of Annie, there is a thing or two I'd like to discuss with you before getting wholly into our session."

"Okay. Shoot."

"First of all, since the cat is out of the bag, are you sure you are still comfortable having these sessions with me while you are technically dating my sister? Because if you're not, I would understand if you'd like to cease our meetings."

Mick gave a look of uneasy puzzlement. "Oh no, I still wanna keep up my sessions with you, Dr. Simmons. I feel as though I can open up to you and tell you things more on a deeper level than I ever could with Annie. I'm not uncomfortable with the idea at all. Are you?"

"No, not really, except...well, that leads me to the second thing I wanted to mention. In all fairness, I think it would be best that we not

mention specifics of Annie in our sessions. It would be too...
inappropriate. Do you understand what I'm getting at here?"

Mick winked. "Don't worry, Dr. Simmons. I totally understand what
you're getting at. Just so you know, I feel the same way, too."

CHAPTER THIRTEEN

I felt such great relief that the burdening secret between Annie, Mick and I had been lifted. I only wished it could have lasted just one more week.

"Which dress, Greg, the black or the blue?"

"I don't care, honey. They both look great."

I frowned.

"Okay, I like the blue one better."

I had been indecisive the past couple of days about which dress to wear for Trista's wedding. I thought I'd ask my mother for her opinion, but she called and said she fell ill with a bad cold and was not going to be able to attend. Gosh, I thought, she is lucky.

"Alright, Greg, which earrings? The hoops or the one's you got me for our anniversary?"

"Mag, without a doubt, the ones I got you for our anniversary. Didn't I tell you to wear them every day?"

"I have been wearing them every day. But this is a special occasion."

"Those earrings I got you to go with everything. I paid a fortune for them! Wear them every day and get rid of all your other pairs."

"Are you nuts? You want me to toss out all my other earrings just because you bought me a pair?"

Greg flashed a superior grin. "I didn't exactly tell you to toss them. You can split them up and donate them to your mother and your sister."

Trista and Glen's wedding ceremony was beautiful. Even though I didn't care for the girl, I had to give credit where credit was due. Greg and I sat in one of the back pews of the church, as the ritual took place, hoping to catch view of Annie and Mick when they arrived.

"You know Annie. She'll probably be late," Greg whispered in my ear. And he was right. We didn't catch glimpse of her until after the marriage vows were made. She stood anxiously in the vestibule with Mick by her side, wearing a red satin spaghetti-strapped dress, as the wedding party made their traditional march down the aisle to the back of the church.

"Annie, what happened? Why were you so late?" I asked after weaseling my way through a sea of decorated people.

"Just lost track of the time. That's all," she answered while passing an endearing glance towards Mick. "Where are Mom and Ollie at?"

"They didn't make it. Mom called me last night and told me she was sick."

"Still?"

"What do you mean by still?"

"Mom cancelled a shopping trip we had planned for last Sunday because she didn't feel well. She said she had a nasty stomach virus," Annie responded as she threw handfuls of rice at the passing bride and groom.

"Well, that's funny. Mom told me that she had a cold."

Annie shook her head with concern. "I don't know, Mags. That doesn't sound right to me. I get the feeling that Mom really is sick. And maybe it's with something she doesn't want to tell us about."

When we arrived at the reception hall, Annie and Mick were quick to get to the bar area, while Greg and I went hunting for our appointed table. We were directed towards table #18 at the back of the room. Upon taking our seats, another young couple sat across from us and we exchanged hellos. The four additional seats at the table were reserved for Annie, Mom, and their guests.

"Annie thinks there may be something wrong with Mom," I whispered, concerned, into my husband's ear. "She gets the feeling that

Mom might be sick with something she's not telling us about."

"Really? She looked okay to me the last time I saw her. What do you think might be going on with her?"

"I don't know, Greg. I'm sure if something was wrong, Mom would just come out and tell us."

"Right. I think so, too. Sometimes your sister can get really carried away and make mountains out of molehills. I'm sure everything will be fine."

"What's that supposed to mean?"

"What?"

"The comment about my sister making mountains out of molehills?"

Greg let out a playful laugh. "Oh c'mon, Maggie. You know that sometimes Annie can be melodramatic. You've said so yourself."

"Yes, but I didn't mean it in the sense that she makes mountains out of molehills! I just meant that she can be really thin-skinned at times. Annie is a very sensitive person. She gets her feelings hurt very easily."

"If that's the case, then she's making a fool out of herself hanging so closely with that Mick guy."

"Why do you say that?"

"Maggie, are you really that dumb? That guy is a total player. He's probably just using Annie for sex, and when he's finished with her, he'll skip town and move onto the next woman. Annie will get dumped and have her heart broken, come crying to us, and we'll just have to tell her that, yeah, we're not surprised. We knew that things were going to end that way."

I found myself getting a little defensive. "So what you're telling me is that you think all this Mick guy is interested in Annie for is sex? You don't think he could possibly have any feelings for her?"

"No, I don't," he answered forthright. "I'm telling you, a guy like him has no feelings. He couldn't possibly have any genuine feelings for anyone. Not even for Annie. He's a gigolo. A male whore. He's nothing but a robot."

"Don't call him that, Greg. You don't know that man. He certainly is capable of having feelings for someone. He just needs a little guidance in that department, that's all."

"And you really think you can help this guy out with that, Maggie?"

"Yes, I do," I answered sternly. "They didn't give me the 'Best of Philly' award for nothing. I'm the best that's out there. And I intend to do the best I can for all my patients. Mick included."

Greg placed his hand over mine. "Mag, your drive and determination is something I've always admired about you. It's certainly gotten you to where you are right now. But, I'm telling you, you are wasting your time treating that guy. Not even you could create emotions in a lost cause like him."

"Oh yeah?" I said, becoming bothered. "I bet I could!"

Greg raised his eyebrows superciliously. "You do? You wanna make a bet, huh? Okay, Maggie, I'll make a bet with you. I bet you, that that guy Mick will never be able to mention the words 'I love you' to Annie."

I could feel my eyes narrow with disdain. "Oh c'mon, honey. That is the stupidest bet I've ever heard!"

"No, it's not. Hear me out, Maggie. It's what, the end of October now? I'll give Mick until Valentine's Day, which is four months from now, to utter those three little words to your sister. Provided, of course, that they're still together. That gives them five months of dating mixed in with over six months of your therapy. If he doesn't say those words by then, he ain't ever gonna say them. C'mon, Mag. You know you wanna bet me on it. You're always up for a good challenge."

"What's the wager?"

"Umm, how about $200?"

"No way," I replied. "I don't wanna bet for money."

"What do you want to bet for?"

"The chores."

Greg cringed with disgust. "Fine, what's your call?"

I was getting into this. He was right. I could never pass up a good challenge. In fact, I thrived on them. "If you win, I take out the trash for a whole month. If I win, you do all the dry-cleaning and vacuuming for a whole month."

"Deal," he responded.

We shook hands.

I gazed candidly at my sister and her new lover. They, by far, were the most attractive couple at the reception, even out glowing the bride and groom. Aside from when the meal was served, they remained at the bar area, constantly at each others' side, laughing, touching, whispering into one another's ear. They were so engrossed within each other that they spent little time socializing with anyone else, Greg and me included.

It wasn't until a popular, slow song by Shania Twain was playing that I'd even had the opportunity to mutter more than a few words to Mick, whom I felt was acting aloof towards me the whole evening. I credited that to the fact that perhaps he truly felt uneasy about my being there; his therapist peering owlishly at him as he wooed her sister.

So, I'm not sure if it was Mick or I who felt more awkward when Annie and my husband decided to switch partners, throwing us into each others' arms, in the middle of that slow crooning tune. We remained quiet as we danced together, which only heightened my ability to notice the way Mick felt, and smelled, and moved. He had a firm, sinewy body, and his arms felt strong around my waist. His hips swayed in a sensual rhythm as the music played on. The dewy warmth from his skin enhanced the musky scent of his cologne and in some instances, I could catch the sweet smell of wine from his breath, which tickled the back of my neck as it escaped his mouth. In a deliberate effort to abstain from eye contact, I laid my head low upon his chest, listening to the brisk pounding of his heart as he drew in slow, shallow breaths. I felt highly turned on, and that frightened me; which in turn, exacerbated my nervousness.

When the song ended, we disengaged and looked into each other's eyes. I never noticed how beautiful his eyes truly were. Gorgeous flecks of gold radiated from them and they were adorned with long wisps of dark lashes.

He lifted my one hand and planted a soft kiss on the back of it. "Thank you for the dance, Dr. Simmons. You look very beautiful tonight. And you're wearing blue. Blue's my favorite color."

Before I could find a reply for Mick's remark, Annie had snuck up behind me.

"Isn't Mick the best dancer, Mags?" she asked with a slightly drunken slur to her speech.

"Yeah, he's wonderful," I answered her.

"Anyway," she went on, "while I was dancing with Greg, I mentioned to him about the two of you going with Mick and I over to the M.P. Lounge when we leave here. Greg's all for it, so as soon as the cake's cut, we'll cut outta here and continue the party elsewhere!"

On the ride to the M.P. lounge, I started bitching to my husband that I was not interested in going anywhere else but home for the rest of the night.

"Maggie, quit being an old lady."

"I'm not," I spoke sourly. "I'm just not into the bar scene. You know that. Plus, we really should be getting home to pick up Derek from your sister's."

"Hun, we're not just going to a bar. We're going out to hang out with your sister and her new boyfriend for awhile. I'm shocked at you! I thought you'd be all for that. And as far as Derek is concerned, he's okay at Carol's place. I swear, sometimes, it's like you don't like it when he's at my sister's house. She does have four kids of her own. It's not like she doesn't know what the hell to do with him. And for Christ's sake, Maggie, it's not like Derek's a baby anymore. He'll be thirteen next week!"

The bar was just as it was when we were there a few weeks earlier,

THE CARDHOLDER

loaded with people, smoke, and loud music. The four of us sat at the last of the empty tables, the one standing next to the blaring speaker.

"Drinks are on me," Mick yelled as a barmaid approached our table. "Hello Sara."

"Hello there, Mick," the barmaid answered snidely, pushing her dark-rimmed glasses above the bridge of her gumdrop nose. "I'm surprised to see you here. I thought you requested the whole evening off."

"Just stopping by for a few drinks with some friends, that's all. I had a wedding to go to. For one of Annie's friends."

Annie flashed a congenial grin to the barmaid, whose face remained expressionless in return. We gave our drink orders to Sara and she trotted back behind the bar.

Annie leaned in towards me and yelled her whisper. "I don't like that barmaid at all. She stares at me a lot. And at Mick, too. I don't know what's up her ass, but she gives me the friggin' creeps."

After Sara returned to the table with our drinks, Annie grabbed Mick's shoulder and spoke closely to his ear. I watched as his eyes fixated on the temperamental barmaid.

"Don't worry about her, Annie. She's harmless," I heard him answer her.

Striking up a conversation was difficult with the earsplitting music on top of us. It was karaoke night and Mick was anxious to fill out a slip and tried coaxing Annie, Greg, and I to do the same.

"No way!" I replied.

"What's the matter, Dr. Simmons? Can't you sing?"

Annie laughed. "Oh Mick, you don't have to call my sister Dr. Simmons anymore! You can just call her Maggie from now on. Is that alright with you, Mags?"

What the hell could I say? "Sure, that's fine."

"That's okay, I like calling her Dr. Simmons better," Mick winked as he rose to hand in his slip to the D.J..

"Oh, shit," Annie whined.

"What's wrong?" Greg and I asked in unison.

101

"I'm outta cigarettes. And I need some damn quarters for the vending machine. But, I feel if I get up, the whole room will start spinning. Weeee!!!"

Greg laughed. "Annie, you better lay off of those shots for the rest of the night!"

I rolled my eyes. "Stay here, Annie. I'll get you your cigarettes."

I walked over to the bar in search for someone to break my dollar bills into quarters. Sara quickly appeared in front of me. "Can I help you?"

"Yeah, I was wondering if you could give me some quarters for the vending machine?" I handed her a five-dollar bill.

"Sure," she replied and proceeded to open her cash drawer to make change. "Your name is Dr. Simmons, right?"

"Yes. How did you know?"

"And that girl, Annie, over there is your sister, right?"

"Yes."

She placed the quarters into my hands. "I know because Mick tells me everything. Maybe even things he's never told you. I know that you are his shrink. And I know what he is seeing you for. I can help you, ya know."

"What do you mean, you can help me?"

"Mick's a pretty complex puzzle. But I know all the pieces to his brain. I can help you figure him out."

"I'm sorry," I explained. "but, whatever I discuss with Mick remains confidential between the two of us."

Sara's lips curled to form a conspiratorial smile. "Of course, I understand that. I could help you out without you even telling me a word. I could do all the talking. And if you care at all about that sister of yours over there, I know you'd like to listen to what I have to say."

CHAPTER FOURTEEN

The chill in my bones sent quivering vibrations throughout my body. I wasn't sure if it was due to the seasonal change in the air or from the coldness that emulated from Sara's harsh gaze. An unidentifiable oddness about her gave me an eerie feeling, but I certainly was not going to let her know it.

I watched her light up and take an inhale of her super-skinny cigarette. We both took a seat on a thick, metal bench just outside the lobby of the hotel. A soft light from a nearby lamp post fell on us.

"No thanks, I don't smoke," I replied when she offered an unfamiliar named box of cigarettes my way.

"That's good," Sara said with an insipid smile. "I used to smoke maybe five cigarettes a day. Now, I'm up to a full pack a day. Thanks to Mick. The stress from heartbreak will do that to you."

My eyes widened. "Were you and Mick an item at one time?"

"No, I wouldn't exactly call us that. I had a thing for him, though, at one time. I was crazy about him. Mickey Dillon could do no wrong in my eyes. If you asked him how he felt about me, he'd tell you that I wasn't really his type. Funny, I betcha he didn't think that on the nights he took me home to fuck me."

Sara was silent for a moment, increasing her number of puffs per second from her shrinking nicotine stick. I could see that she also shivered from the chill of the night.

"I'm sorry, Sara, but I don't exactly know what it is that you brought me out here to tell me. Are you suggesting that Mick may cheat on my sister with you?"

Sara's eyes fastened firmly onto mine. "Not exactly. What I'm trying to tell you is that I was lucky. I got off easy. Just being addicted to a pack of cigarettes a day and all."

I was still confused. "Was lucky? Got off easy?"

"Yeah," Sara responded, flicking her glowing bud towards the parking area. "Lucky I didn't get it as bad as Jen Harris did. That girl took it really bad."

"It? What do you mean by *it*?"

Concern and pain billowed up into Sara's pupils. "*It* is that thing Mick can do to you. It's that feeling of an emotional high he gives to you when he's around. Mick has some invisible inner magnet that just sucks you into him, and once you get a feel for that high from him, you just want more. Mick's magnetism becomes like a drug, and that high can make you fall blindly in love. He can quickly become the moon and the stars, and the whole entire world to you. It's an amazing, beautiful experience that I can't even fully put into words."

"Seems like you're doing pretty good so far," I blurted out involuntarily.

Sara broke our eye contact, turning her gaze towards the parking lot.

Her voice lowered. "There is a bad side to the 'it'. As wonderful as it can make you feel on one hand, it has the power to crush you on the other. When the light that once washed over you from Mick diminishes, your world can become very dark. You can become desperate. You'll try anything to get back into his light."

"Ending a loving relationship is painful," I spoke in a comforting tone. "When one person loses the love from another, it's normal to go through the stages of grief. The feelings associated with the loss of love are very similar to the feelings that arise from the death of..."

"Lady, aren't you *listening* to what I'm trying to tell you?" snapped Sara. "I'm not talking about normal love stuff here! Pay better attention to what it is that I'm putting you wise about!"

I was stunned by her sudden outburst, to say the least. One thing was certain because of it, she really had my total and undivided attention now.

"Dr. Simmons, I don't think you fully realize the importance of your task in helping Mick Dillon fall in love."

I was baffled. "How is it that you know the basis of our therapy sessions?"

"Like I told you in the lounge, Mick tells me everything."

"Okay, and who, again, are you? And what exactly do you have to do with the private sessions I hold between myself and my patient?"

"Who am I? I'm a survivor," Sara spoke with haste. "And if you would keep your bloody trap closed for a few moments and open your ears, maybe you'll understand why I've brought you out here in the first place."

Bloody trap? Boy, this tiny bitch was pissing me off. There was obviously something she needed to get off her damn chest, so I did keep my "trap" shut so she could get on with whatever she had to say.

A dark cloud of seriousness shadowed upon Sara's face as she gathered her thoughts. "As I was saying, if you've ever been the apple of Mick's eye and suddenly lost your place there, there is no worse feeling on this earth. The so-called love experience you feel from a guy like Mick is like no other in this world. It goes beyond the realm of what love should be....and sends you into madness. And you might think I'm just plain crazy in saying this from my own experience. But, I'm not. I've seen what Mick's it has done to several starry-eyed women. Particularly, to Jen Harris."

"Jen Harris fell head-over-heels in love with Mick the moment she laid eyes on him, as have most of his victims. I watched as he wooed her, turning up the charm to levels only he can. They dated nearly a year. They were both very happy. Then, the inevitable happened to her as did for the others. Just when you have tasted and surrendered yourself to the ungodly beauty that Mick has brought into your soul, it gets ripped out of you by his inability to understand the strength of his own power. These women become captivated by him, turning into desperate love junkies, and in turn end up smothering him, becoming jealous of any woman that even looks at him. And, in many instances, I've seen the green-eyed beast within rise out of these once, demure, innocent girls. The complete and utter desperation that inevitably overtakes these women always pushes Mick away. And, I can't blame him for being scared by it, really."

I understood that unexplainable *it* factor that Mick possessed and of which she spoke. I certainly sensed the it when first meeting him, and Annie had totally drenched herself in Mick's it from the day she met him as well. Hell, to be honest, she practically drowned herself in his it!

"The sad thing is what becomes of these girls. I've seen them become alcoholics, drug addicts, junkies, and develop eating disorders before my eyes. All starved for Mick's affection, that he no longer seemed able to return. Jen Harris became a twisted combination of an anorexic, alcoholic, and drug abuser after she lost her spot in Mick's heart. She came here repeatedly, several weekends for months. I watched as the once youthful beauty turned quickly to a wasted wreck of scrawny skin and bones. The mere sight of her frightened Mick. She was a constant reminder to him of the failure he had become to her, and he avoided being around her at all costs. This only made her fall deeper into her depression. She was admitted to hospitals several times for attempting suicide. Then, one night, she managed to take too many pills, and she finally was granted her death wish. All the while she made a point of leaving poor Mick to blame in the suicide note she'd left behind."

I could see that Sara was reading my face for a reaction. I don't know what my face said, but my tongue was certainly stunned.

"The ghost of Jen Harris haunts Mick on a daily basis," she continued. "It eats away at the inside of him knowing that he was the cause of her death. He feels her blood on his hands and is totally devastated by it."

"When did this happen? When did this girl die?" I asked.

"About a year ago. Just a few short months before he met Alexis. He adored Alexis, which is the reason he started seeing you. He didn't want to inflict anymore pain or hurt anyone else like he'd done to Jen and the others. He wanted to learn to use his feelings the right way, as in how-to-give and how-to-receive."

I thought for a moment. "That all makes sense. Wow."

"But now," Sara spoke with a fiery tone, "things will be much worse for him because of Alexis' death. Mick feels as though her death is his fault, too. He thinks she committed suicide because she may have known about him seeing your sister, which may have devastated Alexis. He's terrified right now, to the point where I think he's paranoid."

"Paranoid about what?"

Sara let out a soft, emotionless grunt. "Paranoid that the pain he inflicted on Jen Harris and Alexis LeNoir will also happen to Annie. I see the fire he has in his eyes for Annie. It burns brighter than I've ever seen for anyone. But, now wait... funny thing. I can also see a fire in his eyes when he speaks of you. It's a shame you're married, Dr. Simmons. To have to miss out on an opportunity to be with Mick even just once is a pity. The way he can touch and make a woman feel is quite an experience. An experience that would be remembered for a lifetime."

I gulped, feeling a tickling rush go down my spine.

Sara spoke sternly. "Don't let Mick's potential feelings for Annie falter. You need to help him as best you can to learn about love. Do whatever it takes. I can't bear the fact of watching anymore pained women destroyed. Save your sister. Save the dozens of lives of future women out there. Their fate is in your hands."

I gave her a nod of understanding. "Thank you for your insight, Sara. It's just... I don't understand where you are coming from in all of this."

"I care about Mick."

"Do you still harbor deep feelings for him?"

She smiled auspiciously. "Yes, in a way. I guess you could say I love him from afar. And that is...what keeps me a survivor."

"Hey!" yelled a man from behind. It was Mick.

Sara leaned in towards me and whispered. "Please, Dr. Simmons, keep what I've told you between us. Mick would kill me if he knew I told you about..."

"About what?" Mick said, suddenly standing before us.

He stared at Sara with quizzing eyes. "Why are you out here with Dr. Simmons, Sara?"

"We're just catching a smoke break, that's all."

"Funny," Mick retorted. "Dr. Simmons doesn't smoke. Ain't I right about that, Dr. Simmons?"

"Sara was just asking me about my earrings," I lied. "The noise was so loud inside that she asked me to step outside while she took her break so I could tell her about my jeweler without having to yell."

Mick didn't take his eyes off Sara. His eyes looked cold, and I wondered if it was because he may have figured out the true topic of our conversation. I could sense Sara's nervousness, and I felt bad for her.

"Well, I guess we should all head back inside," I suggested, hoping to break the sudden tension in the air.

"Yeah," Sara said rushing to her feet. "My break time is over and I need to run to the bathroom before I get back behind the bar. See you both inside."

She fled from us quickly.

I rose from my seat and was about to make my way back into the hotel, when Mick pulled at my elbow.

Startled, I turned towards him and he looked intently into my eyes. "Dr. Simmons, I don't know anything about what Sara may have told you out here, but don't ever believe anything she says. She's looney. Whacked up in the head. Sometimes she likes to start trouble. You know what I mean?"

"Sure," I answered, which helped his eyes relax.

The significance of my conversation with Sara loomed heavily on my mind for the rest of the evening. Was Sara being truthful about her stories of Mick's worries, and if not, what would be her motive in making them up? For me to help him fall in love with her in the end?

THE CARDHOLDER

What was the real nature of their relationship?

I tried not to puzzle myself too much with that. I had a bigger problem to work on, the relationship that was blooming between he and Annie. And, unbeknownst to me at the time, the deviant relationship that was brewing between he and I.

CHAPTER FIFTEEN

I thought I was losing my mind. When I heard the incessant barking of a dog, I could have sworn the sound was coming from the back of my house. I laughed to myself as I got out of my car, Derek's birthday cake in hand, and walked up the driveway. My private laughter ceased when I realized that, in fact, I really did hear the sound of a dog barking coming from my back yard.

"What's going on?" I asked, popping my head around from the side of the house.

Derek ran over to me with a huge grin splashed on his face. "Hey Mom! Isn't he cool? Dad gave him to me for my birthday."

A mid-sized Golden Retriever trotted happily along the outer edges of my wilted garden bed, chewing voraciously on a muddied tennis ball.

"His name's Barney," said Derek. "Come over and pet him. You'll love him. He's really nice."

The dog playfully made his way over to me, tail wagging, nose sniffing at my crotch. But, I wasn't interested in meeting the dog. I was trying to keep my cool.

"Where's your father?"

"Inside. Why?"

I didn't answer my son. I'm sure he knew what I wanted to speak to his father about. There was no need to upset him.

I went into the kitchen, where I found Greg peering into the refrigerator. I dropped my keys and the birthday cake box hastily on the counter, a noble woman's way of warning her man that she is pissed and there's trouble ahead.

Greg closed the refrigerator door gently, but did not turn to face me. "Okay. What's the problem?"

"Don't act stupid with me," I snapped.

He turned towards me. "Mag, if this is about the dog, you really shouldn't get yourself worked up about it."

"What do you mean I shouldn't get myself worked up about it? You had NO right bringing that thing into MY house without asking me about it first! You know how I feel about having a dog!"

"It's for Derek. For Christ's sake Maggie! He's a kid. Let him enjoy having the dog. He's always wanted one. It's no problem. Why do you have to go and make a big deal out of this?"

"Because it is a big deal, Greg. Do you know all that's involved in taking care of a dog? Do you?"

"Relax, Maggie. Barney's a year old already. He's already been trained and house-broken."

"Damn it, Greg, there's a hell of a lot more responsibility to owning a dog than just training it to shit outside! He's got to be given food and water everyday, taken for walks, there will be dog shit outside on our deck, in my garden, dog hair on our clothes and our furniture, muddied paw-prints on my carpet, loud barking at night. And what about having to find someone to watch it if we'd ever want to go away for a few days. Jesus! I really don't need the added responsibility of having that animal here."

"It's gonna be Derek's dog. I'm sure he'll be able to take care of him just fine."

"I love my son dearly, Greg, but he's not exactly the most responsible kid in the world. I'm constantly picking up after him like he's a baby. And I'm sure the same will go for everything that comes with owning this dog, too!"

Greg was quiet in response, his eyes transfixed over my shoulder. I was afraid to turn around.

"I'm sorry that I always make things messy around here for you, Mom," Derek spoke somberly. "I'll do better. I'll do whatever you want. Just please don't be mad at Dad about Barney. He's the best present I've ever gotten. Don't make me give him back."

I felt like the damn devil. It seemed that when it came to simple matters with our son, I was always the one who looked like the devil and Greg always came out looking like Superman.

"Derek, if you truly want that animal here, you have to swear to me that you will walk him, feed him, and clean up after him everyday. Do I make myself clear?"

He glanced at his father. "Yes, Mom. I swear."

I cocked a half-smile and gave my son a hug. "I love you, Der. I'm just trying to do what's best for us. And I just can't believe that my baby is thirteen years old today."

"Yeah, umm... by the way, Mom. Could you, like, let up on the 'my baby' stuff when my friends get here. I really don't want to be humiliated in front of them. Especially in front of the girls."

"Don't worry, Derek," Greg said playfully. "I'll make sure Mom is locked up in her cage while your friends are here for your party."

I had asked Derek if he wanted to do anything special for his birthday. Thirteen was a weird age, and I wasn't about to suggest something because I'm sure Derek would have shot down my suggestions by calling them "lame," his usual response to anything I suggest. He came up with the idea of just having a few school friends over to listen to music and shoot pool in the recreation room.

As far as I knew, there would be a few school friends and his two favorite cousins coming over, and I figured on maybe seven or eight kids. So, I was pretty shocked when we had seventeen kids show up! Even though I could easily order enough pizza to be delivered, I knew I'd need more snacks and beverages. I headed out to my car to make a quick trip to the store. As I pulled out of my driveway, I noticed Jill Coopersmith peeping at my house from her front door. I avoided looking at her for fear she would flag me down. I was on a mission and didn't have time to play the gossiping game.

I also felt bad that Derek had not invited her son, Doug, to the party. I insisted that Derek be nice and invite him over, but Derek whined that his friends would think he was "lame" for having the fat, geeky kid there. It was simply not my place to argue.

So, I was relieved Jill didn't nab me on my way out.

Unfortunately, she did succeed in nailing me on the way back. I pulled into my driveway and found Jill peering into my backyard.

"Cute dog!" she yelled in my direction as I popped out of my car. "What's its name?"

"Barney," I answered, wondering what she was doing at the top of my driveway.

"I just walked Dougie over here," she said, answering my thought. "I knew it was Derek's birthday and Dougie had a gift for him, so... Derek's having a little birthday party here right now, huh?"

I felt smaller than the stones I stood upon. "Yeah, he just wanted a couple friends over from school. And he has his cousins here, too. That's all."

Jill walked towards me to meet me at the steps to my side door. "And cute little Barney, here. Derek got him for his birthday, too?"

"Yeah. Greg got it for him. For some reason, he thought it would be a great idea to give Derek his own dog."

Jill smiled. "How nice. I saw the guy that dropped him off this morning. He looked like the same hottie that was living with Alexis LeNoir before she died. Was that who brought you the dog?"

Odd, I thought. "No, I wouldn't think so. Why would you think that?"

"No reason," she spoke with her shrill voice. "Just thought it looked like the same guy. There aren't too many men who look like that around here. Plus, it looks a lot like one of the dogs Alexis LeNoir owned. Have you heard what everyone's been saying around here?"

Uh-oh. Here goes a round of gossip. "No, about what?"

"People are talking and thinking that Alexis LeNoir...she was probably murdered!"

"What? I thought they ruled her death as an accident."

Jill's high-pitched voice turned down to a whisper (she did that when dishing major dirt). "Yes. They ruled it an accident, but according to some stuff I've been hearing, something sounds fishy."

"Like what?"

"Well, I heard something from Holly Mathers, who knows Pam Cassidy, whose brother-in-law Bill used to be Alexis' financial advisor. Apparently, Bill had been fired from being the personal accountant to Alexis' fortune just months after she got involved with that young fellow. He said he noticed that Alexis was taking many small chunks of money out of her trust funds, which he thought was quite unusual for her. When he asked her what she was doing with the money she'd been taking out, she became furious with him, and ended up firing him on the spot without warning. Police interviewed him and they're speculating that there's maybe a couple million dollars unanswered for. No one knows what she's done with it."

"And then there's Colette Jones' husband, who works in the police force, claiming that they probably couldn't get enough evidence against that guy Mickey Dillon even if he did kill her. They say homicidal drowning is very hard to prove. And since the guy lived with her, it would only be natural that his prints showed up all over the place. The only possible link that could tie him to Alexis, the night of her death, is that they found his semen inside of her. It's believed that Mickey and Alexis had sex just hours before her time of death. Mickey claims he was not with Alexis at all that night and even has an alibi. There's some girl out there claiming that she was with Mickey the entire night. So, I dunno. Sounds fishy to me. How about you?"

She certainly wasn't getting an opinion out of me. "Gee, Jill, I really couldn't tell you."

"I still think it's funny that I would've sworn that was the same Mickey guy that brought you the dog earlier. Then, again, I never really did ever get a good close-up look at him anyway. Just that one time earlier in the summer at Carlino's Market for a few seconds."

"Wait a minute," I said in confused. "What do you mean you never got a good close-up of him? Don't you remember telling him about me being voted 'Best of Philly' for couples' therapist?"

Jill's face looked like that of a little girl who was lost in the woods. "No. What on earth are you talking about, Maggie?"

"Yes, it was you. I'm certain it was. Mick was speaking to me one day and told me that you recommended he see me if he ever needed to use a couples' therapist."

I certainly wouldn't dare let Jill know that he was actually a patient of mine.

Her face remained puzzled. "Maggie, I really don't know what you're talking about. I have never spoken a word to that man in my life."

Wait a minute, I thought. "How can that be? Are you sure?"

Jill let out a mocking cackle. "Maggie, believe me. I have the memory of an elephant. I don't forget anything."

Now, that, I did believe.

"What's this all about?" she asked.

Damned if I was going to tell her.

"Oh, nothing, Jill. Just my mistake. My mind wanders sometimes. Anyhow, I'd better get these snacks inside before the kids start eating my furniture. I'll talk to you again soon. Bye!"

How odd, I thought, pouring some Doritos into a large snack bowl. *How did Mick come up with using Jill Coopersmith's name as a referral to me if he'd never spoken to her?* Something was just not right. There was, in fact, something fishy about that. My past few sessions with Mick had gone smoothly and he seemed very focused and sincere about achieving his goal of learning about true love. I couldn't imagine his motive in mentioning Jill Coopersmith to me. And, was that really Mick who dropped the dog off this morning? Did Barney once belong to Alexis?

My mind flooded with questions as I grabbed some cola and the bowl of chips and headed for the basement. When I opened the door, the deafening music was enough to scare any parent away.

Nonetheless, the kids looked excited to see me bring some more grub their way.

"Pizza will be here soon!" I announced scanning the room for Derek. "Hey! Does anyone know where Derek's gone off to?"

"I think he went in his room to get more of his music CD's," Doug answered me.

I trotted up the stairs to let Derek know that I wanted everyone to be cleared out of the house by nine o'clock; something I forgot to mention to him earlier.

I swung open his bedroom door. "Hey Derek, I just wanted to let you know..."

I heard the girl, and myself, scream in shock.

"Oh my God! Mom! What are you doing up here?"

I was stunned. And so was my son and the girl he was making out with on his bed. It seems I flung the door open while they were kissing and just as he was about to unfasten her bra.

The girl, terrified, jumped off the bed and quickly pulled down her shirt. She was embarrassed. Derek was embarrassed.

I was embarrassed.

I shielded my eyes with my hand and spoke like Novocain had spilled on my tongue. "I...uh... just wanted to let you know that the pizza will be here soon and that everyone has to be out of the house by nine. Thank you."

I swung his door shut. And it hit me. At that very moment. It hit me that my little boy really wasn't a little boy anymore. He was becoming a man. This meant he'd be doing things that men like to do.

Aside from helping with the food and clean-up, I stayed out of Derek's way for the rest of the day. I retreated to my bedroom and curled up with a good book, and occasionally Barney appeared at my side. I couldn't seem to find the courage to face him.

116

"Please talk to him," I moaned to Greg as he got ready to settle down for bed.

"He'll be fine, Maggie. Just leave him be."

"I know he'll be fine. It just worries me that he's coming to the stage of his life where he may start to be sexually active. I think this would be a good time for you to talk to him man to man about things."

Greg tried to reason with me. "Honey, don't you think you've embarrassed him enough for one day? After things cool down a bit and the time is right, I'll talk to him."

"No," I insisted. "The time is now. What do you want to do? Wait until our son comes home with an STD or says, 'Hey Mom and Dad, guess what? I got a girl pregnant!'"

Greg lay in bed beside me, grabbing me into his arms. He planted a soft, wet kiss on my lips. "Maggie, shut up. Turn out the lights. We'll discuss this another day."

"Fine," I said, flicking the off switch on my bedside lamp. "We'll discuss this at a later time. But, there is a little something else I wanted to know about."

"Oh God, now what?"

"Where'd you get the dog?"

"What? Where'd I get the dog? From the SPCA. Where else would you think?"

"Jill Coopersmith told me she saw Mickey Dillon come by this morning and drop him off. She also said the dog looks a lot like one that Alexis LeNoir owned."

Greg let out a long sigh. "Alright. The dog did come from Mick. It was one of Alexis' dogs that some co-worker of his was holding for him and he needed to find a home for it."

"Why did you just lie to me about getting him from the SPCA?"

"Because I didn't want to get Mick in trouble with you," he mumbled sleepily. "I thought you'd be pissed if you knew the reason I took the dog was to help him out in finding a home for it."

"Fair enough," I responded. "Guess what else I learned from Jill

Coopersmith today?"

As I began to tell Greg about Alexis' missing money and of Jill's never recommending Mick to me, he put his hand over my mouth. "Hush now, Maggie. Shut up and go to sleep. Or I'll have to start calling you Jill number two."

I kept quiet, but my mind wasn't at rest. I was a bit perturbed that Greg hadn't gone in to talk to Derek. After I heard the faint grunting of Greg's snoring, I peeled off the covers to go and talk to Derek myself.

I quietly opened Derek's bedroom door and flipped on his light switch. I thought he may have been sleeping and felt bad that I might wake him.

But, he wasn't sleeping at all. Instead, I caught him in the middle of a masturbation session.

"Wow, that's so cool," Annie convulsed with glee. "I can't believe my little nephew's jerking himself off. I'm so happy! He's a little man now!"

"Keep your voice down, Annie," I said holding steadily to my boat pose. "I don't think everyone in here needs to know that my thirteen-year-old is a self-loving machine."

"Oh Mags, don't be such a prude. If you had one of those things, you'd be stroking on it, too. I know I would be."

"I'm not being prudish," I spoke defensively. "It's just that things have gotten really weird between me and Derek, and I don't want our relationship to get like that."

"*CHAIR POSE!*"

Annie smirked with reason. "Oh be for real now, Mags. It's bad enough you walked in on the kid when he was getting his first glimpse of real tit. Then you go ahead and bust in on him again when he's trying to let out some fruit juice. How can you not expect things to be weird between you two for a little while?"

She was right. "I know. I just wish there was something I could do to cut the awkwardness and tension a bit in that house."

Annie smiled. "Well, guess what? Today's your lucky day 'cause I have a great idea. Thanksgiving is coming up, and I'd like to cook dinner this year."

I almost lost my breath.

"PLANK POSE!"

"Annie, you want to cook Thanksgiving dinner? That's a first. What's gotten into you?"

"Well, I'd really like to do it for Mick, since he has no family here. And Mom and Ollie can come down to meet him. And I want you, Greg, and Derek to eat my dinner as well."

"But, you know we go to Greg's sister's every year for Thanksgiving."

"Yeah, but for this year you'll have to be there for my dinner. Cause it will be at your house."

"Huh?"

"My apartment is too small for everyone. So, I'm gonna use your house."

"And just when were you planning to ask me?"

"PRESS UP POSE!"

"Well, now, see... I didn't really have to ask you. You'll totally go for the idea yourself, because with all of us being at the house it will help break up some of the tension you're having with Derek. Am I just too smart or what?"

CHAPTER SIXTEEN

"**Y**our eyes seem preoccupied today, Dr. Simmons."

"I'm sorry. What did you say?"

"I said your eyes look preoccupied today. Actually, they've had that look to them for the past several weeks. Is everything okay?"

"Sure. Everything's fine."

"If it makes you uncomfortable that I'm dating your sister and still come in to see you, I understand."

"No, Mick. I'm totally fine with all that. I don't feel funny about that at all."

"Good. Because seeing you every week is really helping me. You've changed my life. I think you're wonderful. As a matter of fact, I think you're the most amazing woman in the world. Because of you, I really know what it feels like to be a real man. And now, I wanna help you feel what it's like to be a real woman..."

My gasp upon awakening was so loud, it startled my sleeping husband.

"Jesus, Maggie. Are you okay?"

"Yeah," I replied. "I just woke up in the middle of a dream I was having. That's all."

"That's nice," Greg mumbled sleepily. "I hope at least it was a good one."

According to how aroused I was feeling, it certainly would have been a wonderful dream. I gently climbed on top of my husband to complete it.

I was glad that my early morning started out delicious, because I had the feeling that the Thanksgiving dinner that evening wasn't going to be.

"I thought your sister said she was going to make the Thanksgiving dinner this year," Greg mentioned while I frantically chopped away at the onion and celery for the stuffing.

I let out a forced laugh. "You mean our Annie make Thanksgiving dinner? Are you kidding? I'm sure she means to. But, you know as well as I do, that by the time she gets her little ass over here this morning to get done all that needs to be done, she won't get the bird into the oven until three. And since we have a twenty-two pound turkey, that would mean we'd be eating around midnight. So, I figured, I'd get a head start for her so we could eat closer to five."

"That sounds great," Greg responded, planting soft kisses at the nape of my neck, "because I hate your sister's cooking. Plus, I have to run out for a little while and I'll make sure I'm home in plenty of time before dinner."

"You have to go out? Where are you going? It's Thanksgiving!"

"I have to go to the office for a little while. I'm really behind on a project I'm working on and I could use part of today to get caught up on it."

"But, Greg. It's a holiday. You've never worked on Thanksgiving before."

Greg became aloof. "Yeah, well, I've never had all the responsibilities that go with being a manager before now, did I? Don't worry. I'll be back before dinner. Look at it this way, your mom and your sister will be here soon, and at least I won't be in your way."

At about half-past eleven, my new doorbell named Barney began barking to let me know a guest was approaching the door. I giggled, scrambling to find the right words to throw in Annie's face for arriving so late.

"Well, it's about time!" I blurted out upon opening the door.

My mother and Ollie stood before me wearing stupefied faces.

"Well, my God, Maggie. I don't think we arrived that late. You said we wouldn't be eating before four o'clock!" Mom spoke defensively.

"And it's not even noontime yet," added Ollie, glancing at his wristwatch.

"I'm sorry, Mom. I thought you were Annie. Come on in."

I gave Mom and Ollie a quick hug and took their coats.

"Oh my," Mom purred, scratching the back of Barney's neck. "I didn't know you got a dog! When did you get this dog, Maggie?"

I hung up the coats in the hall closet. "I didn't tell you? Greg got him for Derek on his birthday."

"What's his name?" asked Ollie.

"Barney."

Mom looked puzzled. "Maggie, I'm shocked. I thought you didn't like dogs."

I frowned. "I don't. Long story. Why don't you both come into the kitchen? I was just about to fix myself a cup of tea."

Mom quickly put herself to work in the kitchen, plugging in the coffeemaker and overfilling the filter with a Starbucks French-roast blend. I put some water on for tea and Ollie comfortably took a seat at the kitchen table.

I liked Ollie. If he grew a beard and a little more hair on his head, looks-wise he would've reminded me of Santa Claus. He was a bit wishy-washy at times, often oblivious to major things going on around him. He lived in his own little world which was completely one-dimensional and nonconforming. He wore the same beige color clothing day after day, ate at the same restaurants where he usually ordered the same dish of broiled flounder, and, according to Mom, hadn't changed a thing in his daily routine since the day she met him. He was the type of person who was philosophical about let-downs in life, and he often liked to present his opinions on politics and current events which were usually based on deficient information. Overall, his placid demeanor was quite complementary to Mom's boisterous ways.

"So, where's that wonderful son of yours?" he asked me.

"Oh, he's up in his room, either playing on his computer or talking to some girl on the phone," I answered, placing cream and sugar on the table.

Mom made a sour face. "Well, his grandmother is here. He should come down here instantly and properly greet me."

"Don't take it personally, Mom. It's his age."

"I don't care what his age is. I'm his grandmother and always will be his grandmother. He needs to learn some manners. Where is he? I'll go upstairs and find him," she mumbled heading towards the living room.

"No wait!" I yelped.

Mom turned around. "What's the problem?"

I sighed. "Mom, just leave him be. He and I have been on the outs a little lately, and I don't want to make anything anymore uncomfortable for him than it needs to be."

"What happened?" Mom and Ollie asked in unison.

As if the circumstances of walking into Derek's room twice, at the wrong time, on his birthday wasn't enough, I also had to deal with the growing power struggle that was coming between us. It seemed as though, since he started junior high back in September, his demeanor with me had changed. We argued more often than not whenever the topic of what he was and wasn't allowed to do came up.

Embarrassed, I replied. "Look, it's nothing, really. Just, basic teenager-parent junk, ya know?"

Mom's eyes crinkled mirthfully. "Ah-ha! I know the stuff you're talking about! Boy, do I remember the things you girls put me through when you were teenagers. Dear God!"

I was astonished. "What stuff?"

Mom rolled her eyes in disgust. "Oh, c'mon. You've gotta be kidding me? Staying out late, cutting classes at school, unauthorized sleepovers at friends, sneaking out with boys..."

"Hold on! Stop right there!" I interrupted. "I did none of those things, Mom. All the things you mentioned were all the things that Annie did, not me."

Ollie chuckled while Mom recollected her thoughts.

"Ah, yes, dear. You're right," Mom recalled. "But wait! Now, I remember the problem I had with you."

A sinister grin enveloped her face. "You were the whiny one. Anything you said or did was ALWAYS right. I, the older parent, was always wrong. I could never argue with you. If you didn't get your way, you'd whine until the cows came home."

If I wasn't awake before, I was awake now. *"What?"*

Mom giggled, shaking her head back-and-forth. "Oh God, Maggie, you drove me crazy. Half the time, I'd let you get your own way because you wouldn't shut up about whatever the issue was. You'd analyze things to death so badly you could make a snowman melt from just talking about sunshine."

My jaw dropped and I was speechless.

"Don't worry, Maggie," Ollie reassured me. "It's actually a good thing that you're analytical, being you're a psychologist and all. And if you should ever decide to drop out of the psychology field, you should think about taking up law. I'm sure you'd make an excellent lawyer."

Mom pursed her lips at Ollie's inane suggestion. "Anyway, Sweetheart. I'm sure whatever it is you're going through with Derek at the moment is completely normal. The teenage years are pretty tough for a kid. It's natural he may be become a little rebellious at times, but it's just because he's trying to come into his own as a person. And it will be hard for you, as a mother, because part of you will feel like you're losing your baby. That beautiful gleam in his eye that was once filled with unconditional love for you suddenly gets replaced with the ugly eye of a self-serving egomaniac."

Ollie curled his lips. "Ouch, Pat. That's a little harsh, don't ya think?"

"Harsh nothing! It's the damn truth," Mom spoke with confidence while pouring herself some coffee. "Now, Maggie the best advice I could give you as a mother is to just let your child be himself. Let him make his own mistakes. It's not gonna be easy. You'll want to prevent those mistakes from happening to him as best as you can. But, your job as a parent is to guide him, and be there for him when he needs you. The more you smother him at this stage in his life, the more apt he'll be to push you away. Just let him grow into the man he's gonna be. Trust me. These next few years are gonna be hell."

"Gee, Mom, thanks for the advice," I responded, giving her a hug. "You always seem to know just what to say."

Mom cackled with glee, pinching my right cheek."You're welcome, Sweetheart. Remember, I'm always here for you when need me. By the way, Annie did kinda fill me in on your walking-in-on-Derek incident when we were on the phone last week. Oh my. So, now, where is Annie and this wonderful fella she's been talking about? I thought she'd be here by now helping you with dinner. And where's Greg?"

I guess I had been spoiled over the years spending Thanksgiving with Greg's family because I seemed to have forgotten how arduous a task it was getting that family meal prepared. Luckily, I prepared ahead by getting all the food shopping done knowing that Annie very well may have been ill-suited to be the hosting chef.

"Mags, I'm so sorry," she apologized repeatedly as she chopped lettuce for the salad. "I really didn't mean to get here so late. It was just...Mick and I, well, we were both...we were having such incredible sex this morning that somehow we just lost track of the time and..."

"Annie, it's okay. Enough said."

Mom tiptoed into the kitchen after spending some time in the living room, with the guys, watching the football game. She put her arm around Annie's shoulder. "Oh, Annie. That Mick's a real cutie! I think he's absolutely adorable. I could just eat him up!"

I laughed. "For Pete's sake, Mom. He's not ten years old!"

"Doesn't matter if he's ten years old or thirty years old. He's still too young for me either way, which makes me extremely jealous. So speak up, Maggie. What do you think about this guy for your sister?"

Annie put down her chopping knife. "Yeah, Maggie. What exactly do you think about Mick for me? You've never really told me your thoughts on it before."

"Well, now, I'm not exactly in a place to say how I feel about him for you. After all, I am his therapist."

"That's bullshit, Maggie," Annie countered. "If anything, you are actually in a better position than anyone to give an opinion on this."

I pried open a can of cream of mushroom soup and poured it into a square Pyrex for the green bean casserole. "Okay. You want my opinion? I'll give you my opinion. But, you'll just have to wait until I can actually form one, that's all. It's just too soon for me to tell. I just can't quite read this guy all the way yet."

After all the hoopla in getting the food prep done, I was actually glad to be spending Thanksgiving at my home. The dining room looked so warm and inviting, and it was a nice opportunity to make use of my best china that had sat in a closet for so long. Best of all, was having the chance to spend some quality time and share a meal with my family together. It had been a while since we were able to do that.

I strolled into the living room to pull the guys away from the television. It was so bizarre for me to see Mick Dillon in my house. Even stranger than that, were the butterflies I felt in my stomach when I saw him relaxed, with eyes closed, in my favorite chair.

"Okay guys! Time to eat!" I announced. "And where's Derek?"

"I think he's outside with the dog," said Ollie.

I went out the side door and into the yard where I saw Barney lying on the ground, munching on his paw. He jumped up upon seeing me and galloped over in search of attention. I didn't see Derek, so I figured he probably slipped back inside without anyone noticing. As I walked along the side of the house, I caught a glimpse of Derek's red jacket in the front area of the house.

"Hey, what are you doing out here? C'mon inside. It's time to eat."

"I'm not eating," Derek spoke in a low tone.

"What? What do you mean you're not eating??"

He walked closer to the curbside, looking like the proverbial cat that ate the canary. "I'm not eating 'cause I'm going over Aunt Carol's for dinner. Uncle Dave is on his way over now to pick me up."

I started to boil inside. "Derek, you are having dinner here with your family. You are not going over to Aunt Carol's this year. And what gave you the idea you could go there? Were you just gonna sneak out without telling me?"

"I don't want to have Thanksgiving here. We always go to Aunt Carol's."

"Yeah, well this year is different. Your grandmother and Ollie drove all the way down here from New York to spend some time with us."

"That's not my fault!" Derek snapped at me. "If you wanna visit with Grandmom and Ollie, I don't care. But I wanna hang out with Russ and Petey, and Dad said I could!"

Before I could get a word out, my brother-in-law pulled up with my two nephews inside the car.

"Happy Thanksgiving, Maggie," said Dave. "It's gonna be weird this year without you and Greg around. Carol sends her love."

"Thank you," I responded, still feeling numb from the sting of Derek's hurtful words to me.

Derek hopped in the car. There wasn't really much I could have done at that point without making matters worse.

"I want you home by ten," I told him.

"Ten?" he growled. "It's not a school night. Why not eleven?"

"How's nine-thirty sound? Keep pressing my buttons, Derek, and we'll get it down to nine."

I tried to hide the disappointment I felt in Derek when I reentered the house. But, I never was any good at covering up the heart I wore on my sleeve. Mom's eyes widened with unnecessary alarm when she saw me.

"Maggie, sit down and eat before everything gets cold. Where's Derek?"

"He went to spend Thanksgiving over at his Aunt Carol's," I

127

announced. "Greg, could I speak to you in private for a minute?"

Greg's voice was wooden, and distant. "Not now, Maggie. Why don't you please sit down and enjoy this meal with your family and we can talk later."

"No. I want to talk to you right now," I spoke adamantly.

I pulled him upstairs into the bedroom, because I had the feeling I'd be raising my voice.

"Greg, why the hell did you give permission to Derek to go over your sister's for Thanksgiving when you knew we'd be having dinner here with my family?"

"He wanted to spend Thanksgiving with his cousins like he usually does. Since when is that a crime?"

"Well, he should be spending the holiday with his parents. And my mother drove down four hours to be with us!"

"Maggie, you always blow shit out of proportion. If you were Derek, would you rather spend time having fun with cousins, who were your own age, or to be bored to death hanging around all old people?"

"These *old* people you are talking about are *my* family," I spat. "At least I know my son wouldn't be getting himself into any trouble with my family."

Greg's eyes narrowed with contempt. "Ah ha! I think I know what the REAL problem is here. You're just pissed off that Derek prefers to be with MY family instead of yours!"

"Don't be so pig-headed, Greg. I don't like our son hanging around those two nephews of yours. Those kids are fast and spell trouble."

"Huh? Are you accusing my family of being trash?"

I regretted even opening my mouth. "Look, let's drop this for now. I don't want to be rude to our guests. Let's just go downstairs and behave like two grown adults, shall we?"

"So, Mick, what is it you do for a living again?" Mom asked.

"I bartend."

"Yeah, Mick wants to open his own pub one day," Annie added. "He can write music and he sings really good, too. He told me he'd love to form a band one of these days."

Mick blushed, seeming uneasy that such an intimate detail about him was being revealed. For the most part, Mick remained quietly composed for the rest of the evening. As did I. Occasionally, we delivered soft glances one another's way. But, he and I spoke little, if any words, to each other. It was as if our relationship was inexplicably forbidden to evolve beyond that of our Monday morning meetings.

After dinner, I was alone in the kitchen with Annie. Greg had Mick and Ollie in the recreation room showing off his new computer programs. Mom was in the bathroom. Annie and I were doing dishes.

"Mags, can I ask you a favor?"

"Sure, babe. What do you need?"

"Can I borrow some money until next week?"

"Yeah, how much do you need?"

"Three-hundred bucks."

"Wow, Annie. That's a lot! What happened? Did you go overboard on your credit card or something?"

"No," she whispered. "I got carried away when I went to the casinos with Mick. Actually, this three-hundred I'm borrowing from you I have to give to my friend Charles at work. I told him I'd give it to him by tomorrow, but I just need another week to get it together."

"Come upstairs into my room and I'll give it to you."

We went into my room and I headed towards the closet to retrieve the box holding my emergency stash of cash.

I plopped on the bed beside Annie. "You know, Annie, you should be really careful with that gambling stuff. You could really get yourself in trouble with that kind of thing."

I handed her the money. She stared down at it and remained silent.

129

I pushed a single golden strand away from her eyes. "Are you okay, Sis?"

She lifted her eyes, moist with tears, and peered helplessly into mine. "Oh, Maggie. I'm so sorry."

I held her close to me. "Annie, it's okay. I'm not upset with you for having to borrow money from me. I was just simply giving you a warning about the danger of becoming addicted to gambling. That's all."

Annie reached for a tissue off of my vanity. "I know, Maggie. I don't know why I'm crying. I guess I'm confused by a lot of things."

"About what?"

She sniffled. "I don't know. I guess it's just stuff with Mick and all."

I was confused. "I thought things were going well between the both of you."

"Oh they are," she reassured me. "Things are going so well and I don't want to mess things up. I'm really falling in love with him, Mags, and it just makes me feel really scared."

"Annie, you're a great girl. This is something you've wanted so badly for so long. Roll with it, be yourself, and there will be no way on earth you could be the cause for messing anything up. Any guy would be thrilled to have someone as wonderful as you in his life."

"Thanks, Mags. But, there are things about me you don't know about, that... I'm not as great as a person as you think I am. And I don't want that stuff to come between Mick and me. And then with Mick, sometimes, he says things. Things I don't understand. It's like, sometimes I feel like he's talking to me in riddles."

I knew exactly what she was talking about, as far as Mick's riddles were concerned.

"Remember when you asked me to tape the first conversation I had with Mick? Well, I still have the tape. I recorded a lot of our talks. I just never gave the tape to you yet because there was stuff on there about me I didn't want you to know about, and I wanted to erase some things. But, I can still give it to you if you want it."

I felt a little uneasy. "Annie, just destroy that tape. It wouldn't be right for me or anyone else to hear it. It's not my place to meddle with what's going on between you and Mick outside of my office. What's your real issue behind the fear you have in falling in love with Mick?"

Annie spoke soberly. "A lot of the fear I have about falling in love with him is based on the fact that I know he may not know exactly how to fall in love with me. You gotta help me, Mags. Mick is the most beautiful person I've ever met. In my whole life, I've never felt this strongly about anyone. Not since Sam. I really think he's the one. And, if I ever lost him, I don't know what I'd do!"

CHAPTER SEVENTEEN

"Your eyes seem preoccupied today, Dr. Simmons."

"I'm sorry. What did you say?"

"I said your eyes look preoccupied today. Actually, Harry said the same thing about you when he was here last week. Is everything okay?"

"Yeah, everything's fine. I apologize, Sue. I like to stay focused when I'm here and try not to let my mind wander too much."

Sue Adelsberg bore a grin of understanding. "It's okay, Dr. Simmons. You're human, so you're allowed. You've done so much for Harry and me over the past few months, I'm eternally grateful to you. We even had sex twice this week without me even having to ask for it once. Things are really looking up for us. Oh! Did I mention to you, too, that Harry and I have decided to try to have a baby?"

The pressure on me to help Mick Dillon in his quest to understand love was becoming heavy. I always worked well under pressure, but something about this case was different. If I had to analyze myself, I would have to say it was due to my sister, Annie's, involvement and vulnerability to Mick.

He sat before me in his usual manner, fingers interlocked resting on his lap, a slight nervous jiggle in his leg, and that familiar, fearful hunger that burned in his eyes.

"Mick, today I'd like to discuss with you an important stage in love known as surrender. I feel at this point you have a pretty good grasp of what true love is all about. How it starts, how it manifests itself, and the possibilities it can bring to one's life. But, in order for one to enjoy and taste the true possibilities love can bring, one must be able to surrender to it. Without being able to surrender to the fruits love has to offer, the fruit will never have the opportunity to ripen, therefore, causing the fruit to rot and die."

My choice of wording seemed to make Mick a bit uncomfortable. The tempo of his leg-jiggle increased.

"Are we on the same page here, Mick?"

His eyes fell to the floor and he gently rubbed the underneath of his chin. "Yeah, I think so, Dr. Simmons. I think this surrendering stage is a big problem for me. It seems as though when I get to that point, something else happens to mess things up. As a matter of fact, I'm right in the middle of that mess up point right now with Annie and it scares me."

My heart skipped. "How is this a mess up point for you, Mick? What is this 'something else' that happens to you?"

He placed his hands on his head, proceeding to run his fingers through his hair, and let out an abysmal sigh as he sank deeper into the chair. His eyes filled with an aching need.

"Dr. Simmons, is it possible, to be able to fall in love with two people at the same time?"

The conversation I held with Sara outside the hotel suddenly flashed vividly into my mind.

Then the inevitable happens... to Jen Harris as well as it did to the others... these women become love junkies... their desperation scares Mick and pushes him away... the beauty of Mick's love is lost by his inability to understand it... you need to save your sister and the future women... their fate is in your hands.

"What are you trying to tell me, Mick?"

He cocked his head. "I'm not trying to tell you anything. I'm asking you something."

"Do you feel that you are falling in love with two women right now?"

"I'm not completely sure. That's why I'm asking you if it's possible."

"Is this a pattern for you?"

"Yeah. It seems anytime I feel like I'm getting close to someone, another woman enters my life and I get confused."

"I believe that you can be infatuated with two people at the same time, yes. But, true love, in its most purest form, can only exist between you and one other person. True love can not exist in the form of a trio. There are too many negative factors that would evolve in that type of a situation. Issues of mistrust, jealousy, ego. Pure love can not flourish under those conditions. It may be possible that you truly love one of these women, and the other woman could be merely a distraction. A distraction possibly created for you by your subconscious mind, and disguised as feelings of love. Your mind deliberately confusing you into thinking it's love, so as to conceal your true feelings of fear towards your true love. The fear in your subconscious is in surrendering to the true beloved. This condition is more commonly known as commitment phobia."

"So, you think my mind is actually trying to confuse me by throwing a decoy my way so I'd be too confused to focus on the next stage of surrendering to my real love?"

"Quite possibly, yes."

"Very interesting analogy, Dr. Simmons. Tell me then, how do I tell which woman is the real deal and which one is the product of my mind's distraction factory?"

"A good test in figuring out how deep your feelings are for a person is through the act of intimacy."

I searched the eyes of the man seated before me. "Mick, what is your true relationship to Sara?"

He furrowed his brows. "Dr. Simmons, that's getting a little personal. Don't you think?"

"That's what you came to see me for, wasn't it? To get personal," I explained. "Is Sara the other woman you feel you love?"

Mick looked a bit perturbed at my suggestion. "No. I told you that woman was crazy. I don't go for crazy women. They're not my type."

"Have you ever slept with her?"

"*What?* I can't believe you just asked me that."

"Answer the question. Have you ever slept with her? Remember that whatever we discuss stays right here in this room."

After a little hesitation, Mick answered me. "Yes, I slept with Sara."

"More than once?"

"Yes," he said, trying to hide his humiliation.

"Are you aware of the kind of feelings this girl may have for you?"

He nodded.

"What do you think you're doing to her by having sex with her?"

He looked shamed. "I'm sorry. I've never wanted to hurt anyone. Not deliberately, anyway. I thought having sex with Sara would actually help her feel pretty good since I paid some attention to her. And, in my defense, Dr. Simmons, there was alcohol involved on the nights I spent with Sara."

"Fair enough," I replied. "Mick, you need to know that there are certain sacrifices you will need to make in your life if you are sincere in your desire to be in love with someone. This so-called gigolo lifestyle you've had up until this point in your life, would you be willing to give all that up?"

"Yes."

"Entirely?"

"Yes."

"And what I'm getting at is that this means no more sleeping around with other women. Alcohol, or no alcohol. I've seen many marriages and relationships come into this room that were destroyed by infidelity. Once the trust is gone in a loving relationship, consider the relationship doomed."

"I totally agree with you on that one. I used to be shocked when I'd get offers for sex from these married women. If I didn't need the money so bad, I'd decline their invitations on moral grounds alone."

I didn't know if I could believe Mick on that one. But, by the uneasy look that grew on his face, his manifesto may have been true.

"I never want to relive that part of my life again," he squirmed. "I'm tossing that bad card out of my hand. I want things to be better. I want to be able to love, grow, and have happiness in my life. It's the reason I get out of bed everyday. Knowing I can be a day closer to truly having that. And you're helping me, Dr. Simmons. You really are. I will get that ace in my hand one day. And I'll do whatever it takes to get it."

CHAPTER EIGHTEEN

With the holidays closing in, it meant my birthday was creeping up as well. Usually, Mom, Annie, and I would celebrate it the Saturday before Christmas by going to dinner after a long day of holiday shopping. This year was no different, except Mom had a change of plans for earlier in the day. A missionary woman from some third world country, that I can't recall the name of, was in town at a nearby suburban church. Mom was anxious to see the woman, who claimed she had been visited years earlier by the Blessed Virgin Mary in her garden, which left her with supernatural powers of high intuition.

The line outside Queen of Peace Church was quite long. Fortunately, the weather was particularly mild for a mid-December morning, which helped to keep my patience in check while waiting for such poppycock.

"I can't wait," Annie said, plagued with the excitement of a kid standing in line for ice-cream. "What do you think she'll say about me?"

"Annie, surely you don't really believe in all that baloney, that this woman can predict someone's future, do you?"

Annie spoke with certainty. "Sure, why not?"

I laughed. "It's all a bunch of BS. There is no way that someone can predict a person's future."

"Hey, anything is possible, Maggie," Mom intervened. "I've lived a lot longer than you and seen a lot more than you have. Trust me when I tell you *anything* in life is possible. One of my neighbors, Aileen, visited Sister Helena when she was at St. Patrick's Cathedral and Sister

Helena spoke to her about her dying grandson's illness. She explained to Aileen that the impending death of her young grandson was simply God's will. Now, how on earth would this Sister Helena woman know anything about Aileen's sick grandson without Aileen even mentioning a word about him to her? Who knows? Sometimes there are things in life that there are simply no explanations for. Only God knows for sure."

After an eighty-minute wait, we were slowly were approaching the podium where the tiny woman stood. She was shrouded in dark gray, surrounded by the light of glowing candles, and had an interpreter by her side.

"Maybe, she'll say something about Mick and me. That we might get married one day or something," Annie whispered to me before taking her stance before the eccentric clairvoyant. I tried to lean in to hear the conversation between Annie and the woman, but was kept at bay by an usher, who explained that I needed to keep my distance from Sister Helena and her current patron, so that my aura would not be conflicting with another. I watched, in eerie silence, as Annie received her reading then stepped away and headed towards the back of the church.

"Go on, Maggie. It's your turn." Mom pushed me.

While in line, I thought of things in my life that Sister Helena could possibly touch on. I basically had everything I wanted in life, and only concerned myself over a couple things. One was the overall well-being of my son, and two, would I ever meet my father one day?

Those thoughts remained with me as I approached the platform to the altar. I stood complacently in front of Sister Helena. She placed her hands, warm with gentleness, atop of my head. She closed her eyes and started to hum softly, chanting words unidentifiable to my ears. I suddenly felt nauseated, not knowing if it was due to the increasingly pungent scent of the incense, or from the thought that this woman may be casting an unknown spell on me. She ceased her humming and relaxed her face. She was a very old woman, whose numerous wrinkles were beyond the help of any face cream. She looked at me with her coal black eyes and smiled, revealing a mouth deprived of many teeth. She removed her hands from the top of my head and placed her fingertips on my cheeks.

"Uhga ruum, batsa meni ta taawla."

Confused at her words, I looked to her translator.

"Sister Helena says you have a great gift of wisdom that you share often with others in need."

"Unh meegan. Su popo tak ootz cowlif gatzhi. Lo kahsents."

"But, be aware. You will also need to keep some wisdom for yourself when your dark hour appears."

Sister Helena's smile deepened.

"Thank you for coming today and may God be with you," grinned her translator.

Annie ran up to me when she spotted me approaching the rear of the church. "So, Mags, what did she say?"

"Nothing much, really. Just something about me having wisdom that I share with people that I should use myself when my dark hour appears."

Annie's face crinkled. "Ew. That sounds creepy."

"So, how'd you do?"

Annie's eyes appeared lost in disarray. "I don't know. She just mentioned something about the water that I'm drinking being poisonous. What do you think she meant by it?"

"Hmpff, who knows?" I responded. "That could be taken in so many contexts. That's what I mean about this psychic stuff. It doesn't really exist. What that woman said to us could mean a million things to a million different people. It's all relative."

"Hey girls! How'd you make out?" Mom moseyed in.

"Alright, what did Sister Helena have to say to you?"

Mom shook her head. "Nothing."

"*What?*"

"She said nothing to me. She said that my aura appeared to be unreadable. And that that can happen sometimes. Oh well! So, how did you girls make out?"

Annie flinched. "She said that the water I was drinking was poisonous."

"You see, Annie!" Mom blurted. "I told you that I didn't like that place where you were living. That damn landlord of yours doesn't look like he cares about keeping up on things there. But, don't worry. As soon as we leave here, we'll stop at a store and get you a water filter!"

Mom and Annie took me to a fantastic restaurant in Olde city named Alastaire's, for dinner that evening. The ambiance was lovely. The floor was made of two-tone marble that was partially covered with floral carpeting, and the high-backed chairs we sank into were covered in tiger-striped fabric. There were fresh flowers everywhere, low-lit chandeliers, and a scenic view of Independence Square from the sizable bay windows.

Mom was in awe. "Annie, I don't mean to sound cheap or anything, but don't you think this place is a bit ritzy for our pocketbook?"

"Don't worry, Mom. I came into some big money when I went to the casino with Mick the other night, so I got you covered. The whole tab is on me this evening so you ladies can get whatever you'd like."

And we did exactly that. Our salads came with a zesty ginger vinaigrette that I craved for months afterward. Mom and Annie ordered Chilean Sea Bass with Lobster Bolognese and I had Seared Sea Scallops in a light mustard cream sauce over angel hair pasta. It was delicious.

"MMmmm, this Shiraz Cabernet is exquisite," marveled Annie.

"Mom, you're not having any wine this evening? I asked.

"No," Mom answered demurely.

"How come? You love a good wine."

"I'm on a couple of medications right now that I can't mix with any alcohol."

Annie and I eyed each other.

"It's nothing," continued Mom. "Just a little problem that will go away soon. So, don't you girls go worrying about anything. I know how you two are."

After our dinners, Annie had finagled the waiter into bringing out a birthday cake for me. I was embarrassed as the nearby diners sang along their birthday wishes to me.

"So, what is it that you're wishing for on your birthday?" asked Mom.

I never really gave it much thought. But Mom was so into believing on hopes, dreams, and prayers, I felt I needed to give her some kind of answer. "Just that all of us remain happy and healthy, that's all."

"I'll drink to that," Annie replied, downing the rest of her wine. "Hey, I got a present for you."

Annie pried into the brown bag she brought in and pulled out a wrapped gift. "I can't wait 'til you see this!"

I unwrapped her gift and felt a sudden rush of nostalgia pulse through my veins. In my hand, I held a framed portrait of Annie and me from a time when we went to the mountains as children. I, around age eleven, was sitting atop of a field with nothing but varied shades of green brushed grass and a gray-white sky in the distance. Annie, about age four, sat beside me with her arm rested upon my bent knee, looking admiringly at me while I blew into a tin whistle. We wore similar cream-colored dresses and had braids in our hair.

I felt warm tears well into my eyes. "Annie, how did you get this? It's beautiful."

She leaned in to hug me. "I though you'd like it! I came across the photo earlier this year and my friend Charles at work offered to paint a portrait of it for me. He gave me one, too! Do you remember when we used to go up to the mountains with Dad?"

"Yeah," I said wiping my spilled tears.

141

Mom smiled. "You girls used to love it when we'd head up there. Dad used to take us twice a year. And you, Maggie, with that whistle of yours. You were always blowing into that thing. If you didn't love it so much, I certainly would've made it disappear!"

Annie and I giggled.

"Hey Mags, do you remember that song that you and I always used to sing in the car on the way there?"

"Ugh!" Mom rolled her eyes in recollection.

"Yes!" I exclaimed. "Wasn't it 'My Darling Clementine'?"

Annie slid her chair next to mine. Feeling the effects of the wine, we put our arms along each other's shoulder and started to sway as we sang:

"Oh my darling,
Oh my darling,
Oh my darling, Clementine
You are lost and gone forever,
Oh, so sorry, Clementine.

In a cavern,
In a canyon,
Extra bedding for a mine,
For the miner forty-niner,
And his daughter, Clementine."

"You two are drunk!" Mom hollered, in a volume level she felt comfortable with in a public setting. "Maggie, you better give me your car keys so I can drive us home."

I chuckled. "Oh, Mom. Remember how much fun it was when we used to go to the mountains?"

She smiled in reminiscence. "Yes. They were some of the most wonderful times in my life. Daddy always looked forward to those weeks we spent up there. After you kids would go to sleep, Dad and I used to make love all night by the fire. It was pure heaven."

Annie's face became serene. "You really loved Dad, didn't you Mom?"

"More than anything in the world. I cherished every moment I had with that man. I was very lucky to have had a love like that, and I always wished the same for you girls to have that, too. It's the absolute, ultimate beauty that life has to offer."

Mom drove us back to my house, where my husband and son were waiting with some old friends of mine for a birthday celebration.

"Surprise!" they yelled when we opened the door.

I was shocked, not expecting it. I was glad though, because I had a chance to see some of my friends that I had not seen in a while. Not until that moment, did I realize how much time had actually passed since Greg and I had gone out and socialized with other couples. The realization that his working hours had seriously jeopardized our social life, along with the amount of wine I consumed at dinner, fueled a confrontation I had with Greg in the kitchen.

"Maggie, why are you complaining about this? Our friends are here now so why don't you enjoy them?"

"Greg, don't you understand the point I'm trying to make to you? All I'm saying is, how long has it been since we saw Stephanie and Matt? Kurt and Jenny? Bob and Katie? Ages! And I think all of that is because of all those damn hours you put in. Hell, Bob and Katie moved into their new house over six months ago and we haven't even been up to see it yet. When are you finally gonna cut back on all that overtime, Greg?"

"Maggie, please don't start that with me."

"And what about us, Greg? Have you forgotten about *us*? How often do we do anything together? When was the last time we spent a romantic weekend away? Huh? We didn't even do a family vacation this past summer! And in case you didn't notice, your son is getting older. He came home with a friggin' hickey on his neck last week. Before you know it, he will be going away to college."

Greg grabbed my arms and squeezed. "Maggie, listen to me. You had too much to drink and if I know you like I know you, you're probably feeling old because it's your birthday. Calm the hell down! We'll discuss the shit on your mind at another time when it's more appropriate."

He left me in the kitchen alone with my thoughts. I began to feel like a total ass for starting a domestic argument in the middle of my own birthday party. I had a pounding headache and the constant barking from the dog in the backyard wasn't helping much. I grabbed some dog food out of the cabinet for Barney in case Derek had forgotten to feed him.

When I stepped outside, I found the cause of Barney's continuous barking episode. He had a visitor from an old friend.

"Greetings and salutations!" I shouted.

"Hey there," Mick replied in a playful tone, stepping aside from petting Barney. "Happy birthday."

"Thanks," I said, walking towards him. "Barney really likes you, huh?"

"Yeah. Barney used to be my buddy. Alexis would always say she thought the dog liked me more than he did her. That's why, when she died, I couldn't seem to part with him. But, when Greg mentioned to me that he was looking for a dog for your son, I offered Barney to him. I was never home and Barney deserved to be with a great kid."

"Yeah, well, Derek really loves him. And, ya know what? I'm starting to, too. At least I can receive unconditional love from something around here."

I felt a little dizzy, so I sat down on one of the steps that lead to the deck. Mick sat beside me.

"Dr. Simmons, I'm sure you are surrounded by unconditional love. Look at you! You're a wonderful person. I'm sure everyone who knows you loves you. Your husband is a lucky guy."

It seemed a little strange to have such a normal conversation with Mick Dillon. It was the first time we spoke outside the office where he seemed to have let his guard down. It was nice.

He reached into his coat pocket. "Here. I have a birthday present for you."

I took a small wrapped box from his hand. "Mick, you really didn't have to do this."

"Just open it."

I unwrapped the box and pulled out a necklace. It was a bit dark outside, so I raised it up to some light to get a better look at it.

"It's a blue sapphire pendant," said Mick. "Blue is a good color for you, so I thought I'd get you something to match with your blue clothing. Who knows? Maybe it will convince you to wear blue more often. It's my favorite color, you know."

I felt a little speechless and giddy at the same time. I don't think I was thinking too clearly when my initial reaction was to give Mick a big hug.

Because, I did just that.

That's when I heard Annie's voice behind me. "Hey, what's going on out here with you two?"

"Oh Annie, come look and see the necklace Mick got me for my birthday."

Annie snatched the necklace without hesitation and examined it beneath the glow of the deck light. "Is this a real sapphire?"

"Yeah. Wasn't that sweet of him?"

She handed me back the necklace, passed a look of disappointment towards Mick, and strutted back into the house. I was confused by her reaction, so I followed her back inside.

After a brief moment, I knocked on the guest bedroom door. "Hey, Annie. Are you okay?"

There was no response.

"Annie. Oh, Annie. C'mon, let me in. I know something's bothering you. Let's talk about it, okay? It might make you feel better."

She finally opened the door, but spoke no words. I could tell she was visibly upset and on the brink of shedding tears. She sat on the bed and I nestled beside her.

"What's the matter, Sweetie?" I asked.

"Nothing," she replied.

"Oh, c'mon. You can't expect me to believe that. What's on your mind?"

"Nothing."

"Are you sure? Is it anything I can help you with?"

Annie's vexed eyebrow gave me the indication that there was plenty on her mind. She finally spilled.

"Okay. You wanna help me? Cause there actually is something you can do to help me."

"Sure, Annie. I'll do anything."

She looked me dead in the eye. "Fine, then. I want you to stop seeing Mick."

"What?"

Her voice was thick. "You heard me, Mags. I don't want you counseling Mick anymore. I don't like it."

"Why? What's the problem?"

"He doesn't need you anymore. He has me to open up to now. If you're still around, he may not feel the total need to convey his true feelings to me. You'd be his intimate confidant."

"Hey, wait a minute now! Just a few weeks ago, you were pleading me for my help in getting Mick to learn about love! And I've really gotten to a point with him that I'm getting somewhere. Now you're telling me to go away?!"

"The situation's changed, Mags."

"How has it? Has he told you he's fallen in love with you yet? Because, last I heard, that hasn't happened."

Annie rose off the bed like a mad hatter. "Listen to me! If you care about me at all, you'll abide by my wishes. You said you'd do anything to help me."

I shook my head. "But, Annie, there seems to be one thing you don't understand. I have no control in Mick coming to see me! All of that is done by his choice!"

"There's a way to go about this, Mags. And don't pretend with me that you don't know how. If you really love me, Mags, you'll do this."

"How?" I asked, afraid to hear the answer.

She leaned in close to me. "Simple. You just tell Mick at his next session, that it will be his last. Because, the fact of the matter is, you feel that he is now cured."

CHAPTER NINETEEN

The holidays came and went. The new millennium arrived bug-free and I finally got to see Bob and Katie's new house when Greg and I attended their New Year's Eve party. It felt good to enter into a new millennium with close friends and my mood was joyous at the initial start of that crushing year.

The beginning of the end, of the person I once was, started on that second Monday in January of 2000. It was January 9th, to be exact. A day I remember all too well. A day I'll relive over and over in my mind for years to come.

It started out as a light, snowy morning in Philadelphia. Driving carefully to work, my thoughts were ensnared in trying to plan my final therapy session with Mick Dillon. I had not seen Mick since the night of my birthday party because he had spent a couple of weeks in Florida, visiting family for the holidays. With the recent progress I'd found in direction to his dismay, I did not feel ready to release Mick from my counsel. But, the pressure to appease my sister from the trepidation that deliberated from her mind was forcing me to do so.

"Good morning, Sandy."

"Morning, Dr. Simmons. Was your drive in okay?"

"Yeah, a little slippery, but fine."

"They're calling for some freezing rain in the forecast later. Boy, Don sure picked a good week to go to Aruba, that's for sure. Patients are calling and cancelling already, including Sue Adelsberg."

"Good grief. She'd cancel if just one flake fell from the sky."

"I sure hope those weathermen are wrong. My neck is still sore from that accident I had in one of those bad ice-storms we had back in Ninety-four."

"I wouldn't worry too much, Sandy. More times than not, those weather forecasters are usually wrong."

I think I had three cups of coffee in that extra hour I had before Mick's arrival. I overlooked his thickened file, determining what my final assessment would be of him. I could hear my husband's voice in the back of my head nagging at me that I would not be able to make Mick say the words 'I love you' to Annie before Valentine's Day. I still had a shot at winning that bet if I could give some quality counsel in this last session. I was feeling quite jittery, but coached myself to be at ease by the time he stepped foot into my office.

"Good morning, Dr. Simmons. And a happy New Year," Mick greeted me with bright eyes and a warm smile.

"Thank you. Same to you. How were your holidays?" I asked while observing the deep tanned skin the Florida sun had given him. He looked incredible.

"My holidays were great," he answered taking his seat. "But, I'm glad they're over. Especially New Year's. I was afraid that the end of the world was coming at the stroke of midnight."

I was shocked, but tried not to visually show it. "Really? Why? Were you afraid from all the talk about the Millennium Bug?"

"I don't know. I just heard somewhere that the world was gonna end, and that terrified the shit out of me. I'm totally afraid of death."

"So, you're afraid to die?"

"Yeah. Terrified at the thought of ever dying."

I decided to pursue that issue a little deeper. "What is it about death that you think you're afraid of?"

"I don't know. I guess it all boils down to the fear of the unknown. I mean, no one really knows what happens to you after you die. Maybe, that's really the end. Maybe, there's nothing after life. Then again, maybe there is a heaven. Or hell."

"And if there is a heaven and a hell, where do you think you'll be going to, Mick?"

He looked uncomfortable by my questioning. "I don't know. In my heart, I feel like I should go to heaven, if there is one. Because I really am a good person. But, on the other hand, the devil may want me because of certain things I've done that have hurt many people."

"What kind of hurt have you caused other people?"

Mick's eyes fell to the floor, along with his short-lived relaxed mood. "I can't talk about that stuff. It's too personal and I don't want to rehash any of it. Just know that, these unfortunate people had to feel hurt from me, but it was never my true intention to make them feel that way. It was just the way the cards fell, that's all."

His piercing eyes met mine.

"Okay, Mick," I spoke somberly, cutting to the chase, "I want to let you know that today will be the day that I'll be giving my final evaluation of you."

He swallowed dryly. "What? What do you mean by that?"

I drew in a deep breath. "What it means is that this will be your last and final session with me here today."

"What? How? How come?" he asked, his tanned face growing chalky.

I leaned into my desk. "Because, I have been evaluating you for several months now and have been able to come up with a prognosis for you. That's what you came to see more for, isn't it?"

Mick's facial muscles began to twitch nervously and the horror that transfixed over his eyes made me feel uneasy. He dropped his head to his knees and yanked anxiously at his hair.

"Mick, are you okay?"

He sat back up, with some color returned to his face. "Yeah, I'll be fine."

"Is it upsetting you that our sessions are coming to a close?"

He laughed to himself, face still etched in desperation. "I'm scared. I don't want to mess anything up. I need your help, Dr. Simmons. You're the only one that can help me. I still feel there is some ground I didn't get to cover yet, and you're telling me that you have a prognosis for me already. How can that be? Was there something I did wrong? Do you not want to treat me anymore?"

I felt a wave of acid well up from my belly. "Mick, please don't take all of this in a bad way. It's a good thing that's happening. Now is the time you get to see the light at the end of your tunnel. I've done a lot of work compiling material on you based on things you've told me in the last several sessions. I have a reputation in this town for being the best at what I do, and I believe that's the reason you sought me in the first place. And I intend to do as good of a job for you as I do for my other patients. You may be surprised what it is I have to tell you. It may very well be the answer you need to hear in order to find the key to your happiness, within yourself, or with the love of your life."

Mick relaxed back into his chair, releasing a slow breath from his body. "I apologize, Dr. Simmons. I didn't mean to sound like I was doubting your abilities. I guess I'm just feeling a little, you know, sad about the whole not coming to see you anymore on Mondays. I always looked forward to coming here and seeing you on Monday mornings."

And I've always looked forward to seeing you as well, popped unexpectedly into my mind.

"So, I guess this is it, then. I'm in the hot seat right now, waiting to be fired at. Go ahead, Dr. Simmons, give me my evaluation. Just make it quick and painless, that's all I ask."

I opened up Mick's folder and pulled out the review I had written up for him over the past weekend. In it, I had pointed out some of Mick's strengths and weaknesses in the game of love. As I wrote my report, it occurred to me that Mick was quite the quintessential definition of a love junkie. He clearly already possessed the key attributes of addictive personality disorder. It would therefore make total sense that he would find phenylethylamine (PEA), the natural chemical manufactured by the brain when we first feel the physical sensations of romantic love, so appealing. Also, by his having what I saw as low self-esteem, the PEA would allow him to feel as close to a natural high as the body would allow. PEA is considered to be a chemical cousin of amphetamines because of the similar "kick" that comes from its secretions through the nervous system and bloodstream that create an emotional response equivalent to being high on drugs. Therefore, Mick may have been subconsciously always seeking out his true love in search for a never ending supply of that high.

"So, you think the only reason I'm looking for a true love in my life is because I want to feel like I'm high on a hormone?"

"Well, truthfully, you couldn't get that never ending supply of PEA from a lifelong love. Your body will only produce that chemical in your system for the first year-and-a-half to three-years of your relationship. This may also be why you keep another lady in waiting, just when you think you're falling in love with the one you're with. You may want to have a fresh supply of PEA that you'd receive from woman number two when the supply runs out from woman number one. Add that to your fear of the unknown, which in your case is love with commitment, and you have a bit of a mess. Don't you think?"

Mick seemed disturbed with my review of him. He rose from his seat. "Interesting analysis, Dr. Simmons. Do you mind if I have a smoke break right now?"

"Sure. You really want to go out into that snow and nasty cold?"

"Do I have a choice?" he asked with a hinting gleam in his eye.

I felt bad for him. "Okay. Since this is your last session and all, you can stay in here. But over by the window. And only crack it a little bit."

Mick lit up his cigarette by the window and leaned casually against the wall.

"Hey Dr. Simmons," he called to me. "I have a question for you. About what you just said to me and all."

"Sure. What's on your mind?"

He motioned for me to come by his side. "First, you gotta come over here and check out this hail that is coming down outside. It's pretty wild."

I made my way to the window. "Wow. I haven't seen hail like that for years. It looks like a bunch of marbles is falling from the sky."

Mick let out a soft chuckle and I refocused my attention from the window and back to him. I felt the sensual tension heighten between us. He took a slow draw from his cigarette. "About that question, now. You say you think I have a fear of the unknown. Particularly when it comes to love. So, why then, would I intentionally seek out something, if I was actually afraid of it?"

"Human nature. We always want what we can't have. The more out of reach something is for us, the stronger the desire becomes to get it. As far as your desire to be in love, I feel that it is there for you. You do want it, but your subconscious pushes it away."

"Why?"

"Did you not understand what I've explained in my report?"

He leaned in closer to me. "I think you're wrong about your opinion of me. I think you actually gave a better explanation of yourself in that report than you did of me."

I was stunned by his inexplicable words. "What? What are you talking about?"

"The inability to surrender to your true feelings because of fear. Having feelings for two people in your life, and not knowing who your true feelings belong to. Yeah, I think that sounds more like you, Dr. Simmons."

I felt my face tighten. "How dare you speak to me like that! You have no cause or reason to state false implications about me. You don't know me. You don't know a thing about me. Did you forget that I am the therapist and you are the patient here?"

"Are you in love with your husband, Dr. Simmons?"

"I beg your pardon! I'm not answering that question. It's none of your business."

"Okay, you don't have to answer it. But, how do you know what the answer really is? How do you really know? Have you ever had another man enter your life that you were curious about? And if that man that makes you curious does enter your life, will it make you question whether or not you truly do love your husband? And if so, how do you go about finding out for sure?"

I was speechless.

Mick continued. "So, how do you find out which one is truly the one you're meant to be with, and which one is the product of your mind's decoy factory, huh? Would you be willing to take the test, Dr. Simmons, or would you be afraid of the results? Because deep down inside, you may be subconsciously playing it safe by not venturing out into the waters."

He passed his cigarette my way. I held up my hand in refusal.

"Afraid to take a puff, Dr. Simmons?"

I was getting annoyed. "No, I just don't like smoking."

"Have you tried it before?"

"No."

"How can you say you don't like something without ever trying it?"

"I don't have to try it to know I won't like it," I spoke with disgust. "Smoking is dangerous."

He laughed. "Well, so is love. Don't you agree?"

With eyes seething, I ripped the cigarette out of his hand and took in a long draw.

"Take it in slow," he whispered in a coaxing tone. "To get the full affect, let yourself feel one with the smoke. Feel it inside you."

I began to cough violently.

Mick took the cigarette from my hand and pounded on my back. "Are you okay?"

"Yes, fine," I replied, regaining my composure. "So, I tried the cigarette. And now I can fully assess that I don't like it. Your point has been made, Mr. Dillon. Maybe you should become a psychologist."

As we made our way back to our seats, Sandy popped her head through the door. "Sorry to disturb you, Dr. Simmons, but the ice storm is headed our way. Marta Jenkins, your last scheduled patient of the day, just called from Delaware to cancel and said it's like a big sheet of ice all over out there. I think the sooner we get outta here, the better."

"I think so, too," I replied. "I'm just going to finish up my session here with Mr. Dillon then head home. Just get the patient files ready for tomorrow and you can get yourself going, okay?"

"Already done. Be careful going home."

"You, too, Sandy. Goodbye!"

"Look, Dr. Simmons, if the weather is gonna get bad, I don't wanna keep you. Maybe we could finish this up next week."

"No, it's fine. I can give my final thoughts for you in the bit of time we have left. Just because Delaware is getting ice, doesn't mean we will."

He sank back into his chair, and I did mine.

I sighed, internally. "Overall, I think your quest in seeking out true love is quite a chivalrous act. Over the months, we've learned about the five stages of love - attraction, infatuation, courtship, intimacy, and surrendering with all its intricacies. We've learned the scientific, religious, and societal aspects of love. I think we've covered everything thoroughly. So, now, as my farewell gift to you, I will give you my own personal thoughts and beliefs on love."

Mick looked at me with reverence.

"Love is a convoluted thing. It has the ability to make us happier than any other feeling in the world, yet can make you feel sadness like no other emotion can. Love is something you can't buy, force, or create within yourself without all the necessary components being in place. Love can be mistaken for many other emotions, until you've truly felt the real deal. Once you've known love, it's easier to recognize. No two loves are the same. Love lives and love dies. You could be madly in love with somebody and think the world of them, marry them, promising to love them till death do you part. For a small percentage of people, that happens. But, for others... eventually the love runs out. And you start having issues, like bills, mortgage and car payments, lifetime goals, how you want to raise your kids, and a whole gamut of other important issues. And all the love in the world won't get you through any of that."

I found myself beginning to sniffle and felt a warm tear trickle down my cheek.

"That was beautiful," Mick spoke humbly.

The sudden sound of sand being thrown at the window distracted my thoughts. I walked over to the window. It looked as if things were icing up outside.

"It's starting to look pretty bad outside. We'd better wrap things up here and head for home before it gets any worse."

Mick rose from his chair and gave me a heart-felt hug. "Thank you for all your help, Dr. Simmons. You've done so much for me and I can't thank you enough. I'm really gonna miss you."

"Hey, I'll still see you around with Annie. And now, at least, you can finally start calling me Maggie."

When Mick stepped out of my office, after our formal goodbyes, I was struck by a sudden sense of loss. I liked him a lot, and felt that, in some odd way, there was some unfinished business between us. I cleaned up my paperwork and gave a call over to Derek's school to see if they'd be having an early dismissal before I left. The dismissal had already taken place a half-an-hour earlier so I assumed Derek went ahead and took the bus home. I grabbed my purse, got my car keys out, and headed for the coat closet.

When I made it outside, I quickly noticed that the sidewalks were glazed by a shiny, thin layer of ice. I pulled the hood over my head and slowly made my way over towards the car. I took light steps, tensing up from the cold wind that blew and the thought of slipping on the ground. I fell twice, gritting my teeth in frustration. When I finally made it to my car, I couldn't get the door open because it was frozen shut.

"Damn it!" I shouted aloud.

It was then that I felt a hand appear on the back of my shoulder.

Mick's apartment was a two block walk from my office. He held onto my arm tightly and we made our way on the icy sidewalks of 8th Street. The slow walk seemed ten blocks long and I felt like a dripping popsicle by the time we made it to his place.

"You know, *MAGGIE*, you would have never made it home in this kind of weather. Those streets are far too iced up and dangerous."

I barely paid attention to the words he spoke because I was too busy basking in the warmth of the heater, which helped the icicles to thaw from my eyelashes.

"You can sit down, you know."

"Huh?"

"I said you can sit down. You don't have to stand there by the door all day."

"Thank you. I would sit down, but I don't want to wet your furniture. Plus, I think I 'm a little frozen still. I don't think I can move."

I was amazed by the tidiness of Mick's apartment. It seemed so unconventional for a guy like Mick to be that way. It almost seemed as though there was a woman's touch to the place. And I knew it could not have been Annie's touch, because she was a complete slob.

"It's a nice place you have here." I told him.

"Thanks," he replied, handing me a cup of hot tea. "I like it here."

"Who picked out your curtains?"

"Annie did."

"Really? I didn't know she was capable of having such good taste. She must really like you a lot."

He smiled. "Oh! Speaking of Annie, she left some of her clothes here if you'd like to change into them. You can take off those wet clothes you have on and I could throw then in the dryer for you."

I gulped down my tea. "Good idea."

I went into the bedroom and rummaged through some of Annie's garments until I found a familiar blue dress. It was an old one of hers that she passed onto me, and apparently took back without me knowing it. The fabric was a little light for this time of year, but figured I'd only be having it on until my other clothes would be dried. I got changed, then called home to check on Derek and let him know that I was staying at a patient's house until the ice cleared up. I walked back out into the living room where I saw Mick standing, without shirt, his eyes widening at the sight of me. I handed him my wet clothes. "If you could just put the dryer setting on low because these are permanent press items."

"That dress you are wearing," he started, "was the same dress you were wearing on the day I met you."

I glanced down at it. "Really? Are you sure? How would you remember that?"

His eyes ranged freely up and down my body. "Oh, I'm sure it was alright. You look dynamite in that dress. And it's my favorite color."

"Blue." I gleefully said.

He put his hand on my necklace. "And you're wearing the blue pendant I got you."

"Yes. It goes well with the beautiful earrings my husband got me."

"Really? And where are those earrings?"

"Right here." I said lifting my hair, heart pounding.

Mick examined my earrings, then danced his eyes upon my face. "You're right. The earrings are beautiful. But not half as beautiful as you are."

I felt an inexplicable rush of emotions.

"What are you feeling right now, Maggie?"

Even though I wanted to, I could not take my eyes off of Mick's face.

"I don't know," I answered him.

He gently caressed my cheek with the back of his hand. I flinched, but it felt good. He leaned in close.

"You don't know?" he whispered, feeling his hot breath on my ear. "Are you feeling afraid at all?"

"No, I don't think so."

"Good, 'cause you shouldn't."

I gulped, feeling the dry lump in my throat. My stomach began to contract like a tight fist and my toes began to curl beneath me. I had to struggle to control my quivering. He stroked my hair. "You know, Maggie, you and I are similar creatures. I know that you love your husband, but you feel an attraction for me, as I do for you, even though I think I'm truly falling for Annie."

"Am I the other woman you were talking about having possible feelings of love for?"

He nodded, keeping his fingers in my hair. "Yes, and I just wanna try and learn what my genuine feelings are for you. That way, I'd know if Annie truly was the only one for me, and if you were just a distraction set up by my subconscious mind."

"Oh, God," I sighed.

"And I know that since you feel an obvious attraction for me, it must make your mind start to wonder what your true feelings are for your husband right now. Correct?"

I felt such a strong overdose of PEA in my system that I couldn't think to answer him.

"It seems that you and I, Maggie, need to know the answers to a couple of serious questions in our lives. Are you willing to take the test?"

His breathing quickened. *My* breathing quickened.

"What is the test?"

"C'mon, Maggie. You know the true test of a person's real emotions . *Intimacy*, Maggie. *Intimacy*. You taught me that."

I felt light-headed. Terribly light-headed.

"Can you surrender to what you're feeling for me now, Maggie? Can you allow me to surrender my emotions for you?"

"I don't know," I mumbled, staring at his muscular chest. "I can't. It's wrong."

"C'mon, Maggie. We should do it. We can help each other out. We can help Annie by doing this. We could help your marriage by doing this. And nobody would have to know."

I felt his warm hand on my thigh, and I pressed my hands firmly on his chest. Then up to his neck. Then to the back of his head, pushing his gorgeous face into mine, kissing him hungrily. I couldn't help it. I didn't know what came over me. He lifted me to him as I wrapped my legs around his lean waist. We tore at each other like animals and my passion for him overwhelmed me. It took over me - mind, body, and soul. He threw me on the bed and quickly jumped on top of me. We kissed endlessly as Mick continued to rub his hand along my thighs. I pressed myself into him, feeling the total weight of him upon me. He ran his tongue along the side of my neck and along the inner part of my ear, sucking and pulling at my lobe as the burning desire for me to have him rose greatly inside. I dug my fingers into his scalp and pushed him down to my breasts.

"I want you so bad," I growled with fever.

We pulled off our remaining clothes until we were nothing but bare skin on skin.

"You're so fuckin' hot," he whispered sensuously while he kissed and fondled my tingling breasts.

I felt like I was having an out-of-body experience. Everything seemed so surreal. I felt drunk with physical desire and there was no way to sober up. Not even feelings of guilt could override the passion that enveloped me. Mick's lips found the lower part of me and I squirmed and moaned in pure delight. He continued to glide his sensual hands all along my body which produced a sweet electric sensation in my veins. The intensity of our lovemaking was too much for me to handle. I felt as though I'd burst if I had to wait for him a moment longer. I pulled him up to me.

"I want you now," I begged, short of breath. "I can't wait any longer."

160

A close-mouthed smile spread across Mick's face and he fulfilled my wish.

We stayed in each other's arms until our breath and heartbeats returned to their normal pace.

"Are you okay?" he asked me.

"Yes."

"Are you feeling guilty right now for what you just did?"

"I'm not sure. I'm confused. I've never cheated on my husband before. Cheating totally goes against my morals and beliefs. Yet, at the same time, I feel... I don't know... relieved."

Mick kissed my forehead. "Yes. And relief is what you should feel. It's how I'm feeling also. It felt good to get you outta my system."

I lifted my head. "I'm outta your system?"

"Well, yeah. Don't you feel the same towards me?"

I smiled. "Yeah, I think so."

"So don't feel the least bit guilty about what we did. At least now we never have to wonder, what if? You and I were infatuated decoys for each other. Now we can stay focused on the true loves in our lives that were meant to be."

"Annie?" I asked.

He grinned. "Yes, I really think I love her, Maggie."

"Really?" I bounced. "Until another decoy comes your way?"

His grin enlarged as he thought of her. "No. It's not like that. Annie is my ace. She's that top card I was looking for all my life. And you gave that card to me, Maggie. I would have never seen it if you didn't show it to me. The next time I see her, I'm gonna tell her that I love her. It wasn't until this very moment that I realized that I truly do love her with all my heart."

I felt overjoyed. Annie was crazy for Mick and I was so pleased that he had, in fact, really felt the same towards her. Mickey Dillon had finally fallen in love.

My work was done.

KELLY O'CALLAN

I stepped out into the pouring rain and headed back to my car.

CHAPTER TWENTY

The warm spray of the shower washed away the coldness of the rain and any residual scent of Mick on my skin. I thought about the final words that Mick and I spoke as I headed out his door.

"So, what is to become of Maggie Simmons after this?" he asked.
"Well, Maggie's gonna do her best to relight the passion that's been missing in her marriage for so long," I smiled.
Mick smiled back. "Good, because no matter what happens to you, you deserve the best."

After my therapeutic shower, I checked my answering machine. Annie called to say she'd be skipping yoga class that evening and Greg called to let me know he'd be bringing dinner home from KFC after work. Feeling a bit exhausted from the events of the day, I decided to lay down for a light nap. I yelled into the family room. "Derek, I'm gonna lay down for a couple of hours. Wake me up when Daddy gets home, okay?"

As I laid down, methods to reignite the romance that Greg and I once had flooded through my mind. I was certainly determined to make something good come out of my unexpected adulterous affair.

***

"Mom. *Mom!*"
"Hmmm?"
"Mom, wake up. Dad's home. And Aunt Annie's here, too. She

wants to see you."

My head pounded cruelly as I tried to lift it from the pillow. I opened my eyes and made out the form of my son standing over me.

"C'mon, Mom. Dad brought home some KFC. You'd better come down before the stuff gets cold."

"Okay, Sweetie. I'll be down in a minute."

I felt dizzy when I stood up from the bed, grabbing my robe from the clothes tree. I went into my bathroom, opened up the medicine cabinet, and popped a couple of Excedrin in my mouth in hopes of getting rid of my nasty headache.

I made my way down the stairs where I first caught a glimpse of Annie.

"Hey, Annie. What are you doing here? I thought you were gonna skip yoga class this evening?"

Annie stood before the couch, arms crossed, jaw clenched, and her nostrils flared. She peered wild-eyed at me and in an instant, I was being hunted down by her scorching stare. I'll never forget that agonizing look on her face. Never.

"You BITCH!" she spat, lips curled in disgust.

"Annie?"

"Tell me it's NOT true!"

I froze.

Impatience crept into her voice. "How could you? You're my sister!"

Greg and Derek ran out from the kitchen. "Hey! What's going on in here?"

I panicked. "Derek, go upstairs to your room."

"But, Mom, I'm eating dinner!"

"I don't care! Get upstairs now!"

Greg watched as Derek heavy-footed his way up the steps. "Will somebody tell me what the fuck is going on around here?"

"Nothing, Greg, go away. This discussion is between me and Annie."

"No!" Annie yelled boldly. "I think Greg needs to hear exactly what it is I have to say. And what YOU have to say."

I shivered. "Calm down, Annie. I'm sure whatever you heard was misunderstood by you and..."

"I don't think so!" she snapped, unraveling one of her clenched fists. "Missing an earring, are we?"

I put my fingers to my ears and felt an empty smoothness on one of my lobes.

"Because I found the mate to it. It's here in my hand. And you wanna know where I found it? On Mick's bed!"

Greg raised his eyebrows. "*What?* Maggie, what *the hell* is going on here?"

"You've got it all wrong, Annie" I tried to explain. "I couldn't drive home because the streets were too icy earlier. I was stuck! Mick was nice enough to let me stay at his place until the rain changeover, and I was only in his room because I changed out of my wet clothes into one of the spare dresses you had left there. The earring must have popped off then."

"What about the test?" Annie's voice strained, thick with insinuation.

"Huh?"

"The test, Maggie, tell Greg and I about the test you and Mick took together."

At that point, I knew I was fucked. I just didn't understand why Mick had opened his big mouth. We'd sworn to keep the incident a secret. My heart sank, and my face must have shown it. I was caught. What could I have said?

Pools of tears formed like glass over Annie's eyes and she began whimpering. "It's true. Isn't it?"

I dropped my eyes to the floor. I couldn't face her. The guilt I escaped earlier splashed over me like a tidal wave and I was drowning in it. "I'm so sorry."

Annie continued to bawl like a baby. "*Why?* How *could* you? How DARE you sleep with MY boyfriend! You're nothing but a filthy

WHORE!"

"Oh my God," Greg mumbled with a pained voice, exiting the room.

"It's not what you think, Annie. Honestly," I struggled to reason.

Annie tried to gain her composure. "Shut up! I don't wanna hear any of your lies! It is what it is. You and Mick had sex, end of story. Do you have any idea how hurt I'm feeling right now? I loved Mick, and he cheated on me. I lost what I had with him now. And you! You're supposed to be my sister! If there was one person I thought I could trust on this earth, I thought it would be you. You were my best friend, and I lost you, too."

"No, Annie. I'm here, you'll never lose..."

"Stop it!" she snapped, raising her hand. "Don't say another word to me."

She leaned over the couch, picked up her coat, and headed towards the door. She opened the door and looked at me with hate in her eyes, her voice as cold as death. "Goodbye, Mags. I hope you're happy with what you've done, because I never plan on speaking to you again."

CHAPTER TWENTY-ONE

The next several weeks and months would prove to be some of the most devastating times in my life. The price I would have to pay for my extramarital affair was undeniably high. A monumental casualty from my ominous sexual liaison was, unfortunately, my marriage.

Greg found it very difficult to talk, let alone stay in the same room as me. At nighttime, he'd sleep on the couch or in the guest bedroom. I felt tremendous hurt from the growing rift I caused between us and would often ask to talk about what was happening between us. Greg would often invariably say that he was not ready to talk about things yet with me. He needed time to let the shock and hurt die down inside of him. I soon saw less and less of my husband. He returned home later and later with each passing night. Until the one evening when he came home and was ready to talk. He told me that he was leaving me because he felt totally betrayed by me and just didn't know if he'd be able to trust me again. I begged him not to go, but he said he needed his space to sort things out.

I had also lost the closeness I had with my sister. I called her numerous times, leaving plea-ridden messages, but none of my calls were ever returned. I dropped in to see her at work, but she always refused to see me. I continued going to our yoga class on Monday evenings, but soon stopped when all I felt was the pain of her absence.

I also lost many patients from my practice, including Sue and Harry Adelsberg.

"I'm sorry, Dr. Simmons. It's just that Harry feels it's kinds silly that we see a marriage therapist who had an extra-marital affair on her husband."

"Sue, where did you hear a thing like that?"

"My nephew. He goes to school with your son, Derek, but I think he actually heard about it from your neighbor's son. Does the last name Coopersmith ring a bell?"

With my tale on Jill Coopersmith's lips, soon the whole town knew of my affair and of my separation from my husband. There was even an item about it in the local paper.

Woman Voted 'Best of Philly' Marriage Therapist Commits Adultery

I had caused such a disgrace, that Don suggested I take a leave of absence from work, at least for a while, so I could "take time to heal my mind."
I even tried calling Mick Dillon repeatedly to find out why he told Annie of our rendezvous. He returned none of my calls.

Then, I had the matter of my son. He, too, seemed to be distancing himself from me more every day. The hardest blow I took from him was when he told me that he wanted to live with his father, because everything that had happened was my fault. At first, I told him that he was going to stay with me, but when he rebelled and Greg threatened me with a divorce and custody suit, I obliged.

So, I was left alone in the house. Even Barney was gone, and he was the only one who still paid any attention to me. My world was crumbling around me. I thought life couldn't possibly get any worse.

Then it did.

CHAPTER TWENTY-TWO

It was a Saturday morning in late March when I received an unexpected phone call from Mom.

"Hello, Maggie. It's Mom. I need you to do a favor for me."

"Sure, Ma. What do you need?"

"Margaret, you sound like complete shit. Have you been drinking?"

"No, I haven't been drinking. But, yes, I feel like total shit. What's the favor, Mom?"

"I need you to go over Annie's and check on her for me. She was supposed to come up on the 9:15 train to meet me for a day of shopping. And she never showed up."

"You know her, Mom. She's always late. She probably missed the train and is on the next one."

"I thought of that already, Smartie. I've been here at the train station for almost two hours! And she wasn't on the two other trains that came in from Philly after the 9:15."

"Have you tried calling her?"

"Yes, and there's been no answer on her cell phone or her home number. Could you just do me a favor and run by her apartment for me? It should only take you a few minutes. I just wanna make sure she's alright."

I hesitated. "I know what you're trying to do, Mom. You're not fooling me."

"What are you talking about?"

"You're trying to come up with a scheme to make Annie and I talk again, aren't you? It probably isn't gonna work. Annie seems to want no part of me still."

Mom's voice became tinged with disappoint. "I think it's absolutely ridiculous that the two of you are behaving like such babies. You should learn to kiss and make up. Life is too goddamn short."

"I've tried to talk with Annie, Mom! I call her, I send her cards and letters, I've tried to see her at work and have been to her apartment. She refuses to see me."

"Well, Jesus, Maggie. Can you blame the poor girl? You went behind her back and slept with her boyfriend. And you of all people. Her own sister!"

"I don't want to go through another speech on this again with you, Mom," I said, filling up with grief. "I've had enough happen to me in the past month. I can't take anymore."

"What's happened, Darling?"

I began crying. "Oh, Mom. Greg left me."

"What? When did this happen?"

"About a month ago. He moved into a place a couple of miles from here. And last week, Derek left to move in with him. He said he'd rather live with his dad than with me. I think he hates me."

My voice began to quiver. "What have I done? I ruined so many things by the stupid mistake I made. My life is falling apart around me and I don't know how to fix it!"

Mom spoke in a soothing tone. "Maggie, sweetheart. I know it's got to be tough what you're going through right now. As a mother, it kills me to see you in pain. I wish I could kiss your boo-boos and make all the pain go away for you. But, I can't. The only thing that can help you now is time."

"I know that, Mom. Thanks, I love you."

"I love you, too. And after these busy couple of weeks I have ahead of me are done, I'd love it if you'd come up and stay with me for a few days. I think it would do you some good."

I smiled. "Yeah, me too."

"Now, can you just do that favor for me?"

"You mean go over to Annie's? Is that favor you're asking me about real?"

"Of course it is!"

"Okay, I'll go over for you, but I don't know if she'll let me in. Did you ever think maybe she's over at Mick's place?"

"I don't know how that could be. She and Mick are split up."

I felt my stomach drop to the floor. "Wha... when did that happen?"

"When you went and slept with him. It's been a couple of months now, huh?"

I felt like complete scum.

"You know," Mom continued. "Annie has not been right since that incident. I've never seen that girl so down in the dumps before. She sounds terrible. You should get over there and the both of you should make your peace. Just call me as soon as you get over there and let me know what's going on."

I parked alongside Annie's car in her lot so I figured she was probably home. She was likely out the night before and just overslept. I walked into her apartment's entrance way, pushed her code into the intercom system, and waited for Annie's breathy 'Hello, who is it?' If I had gotten a hello from her, that would have been probably all I'd get. I had stopped by her apartment a few times in the last couple of months and when she'd learned it was me buzzing, nothing further was said on her part.

After no response, I pressed her number again. And again.

Then I called Mom on my cell phone. "Her car's here. But she's not responding to my buzzing."

"I don't like that, Maggie. I'm really worried."

"Maybe she went out with a friend last night who picked her up and she ended up sleeping over and didn't come home yet," I suggested.

"No," Mom spoke with concern. "Annie was really looking forward to coming up and spending the day shopping with me. Something is just not right. I feel it in my gut. Listen, Maggie, do you have a key to her apartment to get in?"

"I just can't barge in there, Mom! Then she'll really have nothing to do with me for the rest of my life."

"I really don't give a damn right now if she'd be pissed at you for the rest of your life or not! I wanna know that my daughter's okay! Oh... Jesus Christ, my battery is going dead on this phone. Look, I have to run to a store while I'm here by the station. Tell Annie to stay put. I'll call you when I get home."

I fingered through my key-chain and pulled out the keys to Annie's doors. I unlocked my way through the foyer door and walked down the hall to Annie's apartment. I thought I'd be considerate and knock before unlocking it. I pressed my ear to the door and heard the faint sound of music playing. I couldn't distinguish if it was coming from the radio or the television.

I knocked again and called out Annie's name.

I then heard a door begin to open. But, it wasn't hers. Just the old lady's that lived beside her. She looked at me wide-eyed. "You lookin' for that young girl that lives in there?"

"Yes. Why do you ask?"

The lady shook her head. " 'Cause I heard her come home real late last night hootin' and hollerin' in the hallway as drunk as a skunk."

"Oh, really? Hi, my name is Maggie. I'm her sister."

The woman proceeded to eye me like I was a mutant. "Hello, Maggie. I'm Gladys. You better tell that sister of yours to keep quiet around here late at night. A lot of us older folk don't care for that noisy stuff in the halls."

I quickly slipped my key into the slot. "Okay, Gladys. I'll be sure to tell her."

When I stepped into her apartment, I discovered that the music I heard was coming from the CD player. A song called "Bad Girl" by Madonna, Annie's favorite artist, played wistfully into the air. It was a song I had once liked, but will never listen to again. The melodic tune that once brought enticing pleasure to my ears, would now just inflict horrific pain to my memory. The memory of when I first found my beloved baby sister dead.

I walked into the bedroom where I found Annie lying sprawled out, half naked, on her bed. I instantly noticed her skin was grayish-white in color, and had an odd waxiness in texture. Her lips were blue and partially hidden by some kind of dark, bloody froth that oozed from her parted mouth and onto one side of her face. And her partly opened eyes were cast with a bluish-white glaze that erased the beauty of the vibrant emerald green color that once lived in them. The room also had an indescribable stench to it. I screamed from the bottom of my lungs.

"ANNNNNIIIIIEEEEE!!!"
"ANNNNNIIIIIEEEEE!!!"
"ANNNNNIIIIIEEEEE!!!"

I started to cough and choke on my fast pouring tears, and my tightened lungs made it difficult to breathe. Without warning, instant shock began to set into my body. I became dizzy and the room quickly blurred to black.

***

When I came to, I found myself lying on Annie's sofa, legs propped high, with Gladys applying a damp cloth to my head. There were several strange uniformed men in the room.

"Annie! Annie!" I cried out, pushing Gladys' arm away from my head.

Gladys' face was gloom-filled. "You poor, dear. I'm so sorry. I'm so sorry for what's happened to your sister."

I jumped off the couch and hurried my way past some men towards the bedroom, calling out to my sister. A man with a thin mustache raised his arm and stopped me at the doorway.

"I'm sorry, Miss. But you can't go in there."

I watched, enveloped in horror, as one man drew blood samples from Annie's body, another swabbed the inside of her mouth, and a third stood over her taking pictures from various angles. "But, that's my sister in there!"

"So, you're related to the deceased?"

"No! She's not dead! Annie is not dead! Leave her alone! Don't you dare hurt her!!" I cried out furiously.

The man's eyes grew sympathetic. "M'aam. Could you please come with me to the table? I have some questions I'd like to ask you."

I sat quietly at the dining room table and stared at the space where the floor and wall met as the paramedic took my blood pressure and gave me an injection of something that quickly made me sedate. The man with the Clark Gable mustache flipped the receiver to his cell phone. "Your husband is on his way over, Ms. Simmons."

"Thank you," I think I mumbled.

He picked up a recent picture of Annie and Mick taken at Trista's wedding that sat diagonally atop of the entertainment center. He then sat beside me.

"Nice-looking couple. I remember this young lady and this young fellow. They were both questioned regarding facts to the LeNoir case back in October. In fact, I had questioned them both myself," he spoke.

"Excuse me," my voice croaked. "But who are you again?"

"Detective Colletti, with the Philadelphia Crime Scene Unit. I'd like to ask you some questions regarding your sister, Annie. Do you think you could help me out a bit?"

"I'll try," I responded, taking the blanket offered to me by the paramedic.

He turned to a fresh page in his notebook and pulled out a pen and a recording device from the inside of his vest pocket.

"Ms. Simmons, could you tell me approximately when it was you last saw your sister alive?"

"Yeah, I sure can. It was the evening of January ninth."

"And today is March twenty-sixth. So, you had not seen your sister in over two months?"

"That's correct."

"And what kind of relationship did you have with your sister?"

"That's a little personal, don't you think?" I spoke with offense.

Detective Colletti bore a crooked smile. "Sorry, Ms. Simmons. Just doing my job."

I recollected numerous thoughts in my past that involved Annie. "Annie and I were very close. Best friends, actually. There wasn't anything in the world I wouldn't have done for her. I loved her with all my heart and always will. We had a bitter falling out recently. And it breaks my heart to know that we'll never get the chance to make up."

"What caused the so-called 'fall out' in your relationship?"

"Personal family stuff," I answered, feeling disturbed.

"And what was the purpose of your visit here today?"

"I was doing a favor for my Mom. Annie was supposed to meet her this morning to go shopping where Mom lives in Manhattan and Annie never showed up. Mom wanted me to take a run over here just to be sure... to be sure... to be sure Annie was alright."

I began to tremble, feeling a hot wetness pool into my bleary eyes. Everything seemed unreal.

"Ms. Simmons, could you identify the man in the picture here with Annie?" the detective asked holding the picture my way.

"Yes. That's Mickey Dillon, Annie's boyfriend. Well, ex-boyfriend."

Detective Colletti scribbled some notes onto his pad. "This Mickey Dillon fellow. Could you tell me what he's like? And maybe what kind of relationship he and your sister had together?"

I became alarmed. "Why do you ask, Detective Colletti? Do you think he has something to do with Annie's dying?"

"I'm not sure," he answered with a furtive look. "I can't rule anything out at this point. Just want to get some facts together. Annie's neighbor gave a statement earlier noting that Annie had come home somewhere between midnight and one o'clock this morning accompanied by a tall man wearing a gray suede jacket. I asked if she could positively identify the man as being the one in this picture, and

175

she said she didn't think it was the same man. But at the same time, she also admitted that the images she sees through her peephole are often distorted. To be honest, I find it a bit odd that this Mickey Dillon guy has been linked romantically to two women who've died just months apart. I've got to investigate that issue a little further."

"Detective Colletti, are you suggesting you think somebody, maybe even Mick, murdered Annie?"

"Like I said, Ms. Simmons, I can't rule out anything at this time, including the possibility of homicide. That bedroom is being treated as a crime scene right now. But, I also can't rule out the likelihood that Annie's death was accidental or suicidal. As it looks right now, Annie's death appears to be the result of a deadly combination of drugs and/or alcohol. But, only the coroner's office can determine that for us for sure."

"How long will all this investigating take?"

"Speaking in terms of justice for the victim as well the possible accused, if it is in fact ruled a homicide, this is a process that can't be rushed. I've seen some searches take as short as fifteen minutes and others as long as four days."

"How long before the autopsy is done?"

"Good question," he noted, and with that he turned his head toward the hallway. "Hey Matlin! Could you come into the dining area for a second?"

A thin man with dark, straggly hair appeared. "What's up?"

"Give me an overview of what you've got so far."

"We're wrapping things up now, Detective. Samples and prints were taken. Fixed lividity, clouded corneas, and full body rigidity noted. Photos are done. And now we're just waiting for measurements and sketches to be completed."

"Great," Colletti smiled. "So we can go ahead and remove the corpse upon completion of the sketchings?"

"Yes, sir."

"Good job, Matlin. I'm going to accompany the body to the morgue to witness the autopsy. Make sure you seal up the scene well, just in

176

case we need to return."

Greg arrived just as Annie's body was being lifted onto a gurney. I was sitting on the couch and began to weep like a dark rain cloud when I saw him. He sat beside me and squeezed my body tight in a gesture of warmth and support. He held onto my hands firmly as I told him details of the frightening day.

We looked on as the gurney left the bedroom and entered into the living room. Annie's body was draped with white sheets and strapped down with belts. My sister was leaving her home, her safe haven, for the last time. I rose up from the couch, eyes transfixed onto the unwieldy mass under the sheets of the stretcher. I placed my hand gingerly on the coverlet, feeling nothing but hard coldness emulate from it. That was not my Annie under there, I told myself. She was filled with total warmth and love of life. The matter beneath the sheets was merely an empty shell of death. I fought back my impending storm of emotion but lost, feeling the thunderous undercurrents rip throughout me, leaving me gasping for air. I fell back into the arms of my husband, holding onto him for dear life.

"My sweet Annie! Oh, my Annie! I'm so sorry! *Why did you have to go?* I love you so much! Please come back! Please... come back!"

Greg tightened his grip around me.

"I'm so sorry, Maggie. I'm so sorry," he spoke in a pained voice.

Detective Colletti whispered to my husband. "Mr. Simmons, if I were you, I'd get your wife to a doctor ASAP for some help. It's highly possible that she may be suffering with post traumatic stress disorder after the events of today."

"Thank you, Detective. I'll see to it she's taken care of."

Detective Colletti placed his hand gently onto my back. "Maggie, I'm sorry this had to happen to you and your family. I'll be in touch with you about the coroner's report as soon as I receive it. Hang in there."

My body shivered angrily in the car. My stomach knotted so tightly I thought my insides would violently burst open. Greg drove slowly, stroking me gently at traffic lights. Since the shocking pain we felt had viciously taken our voices, no words were able to be spoken between us. After we pulled into the driveway, Greg walked out and came around to help me out of the car. I staggered my way into the house and was struck by a bolt of alertness when I saw the red blinking light on my answering machine.

"Oh my God, Greg," I said after my sudden realization. "I have to call Mom."

He looked at me, eyes filled with concern. "She doesn't know yet?"

I placed my hands over my face. "No, I haven't called her yet. How do I do that? How am I gonna tell that woman her daughter is dead?"

"Maybe we should take a ride up and tell her in person."

"No, there's no time. I know that's her on the answering machine tracking me down."

RING... RING...

I froze. "Oh, God! What if that's her now?"

"Pick up the phone, Maggie. You gotta tell her."

"No! I can't! I don' know how!"

RING... RING...

"Well, if you don't wanna tell her, then I'll do it," he said, picking up the receiver. "Hello? Hi, Pat, yeah, she's here."

I looked at him, wide-eyed, as I reached for him to hand me the receiver. "Hello Mom... I want you to sit down... I've got some bad news to tell you, about Annie..."

CHAPTER TWENTY-THREE

"**M**ags, where are you? I can't see you."

"I'm right here, Annie. Where are you?" I responded, blinded by the air thickly covered with cloud.

"I'm here too, Mags. But, I'm afraid I'm gonna get lost."

"You won't get lost," I shouted. "Just follow my voice and you'll be able to find me."

"I'm trying," Annie spoke nervously. "But your voice is getting harder and harder for me to hear. I'm afraid I'll disappear up here all alone."

I waved my hands frantically through the white fog. "No, Annie. I won't lose you. I'm going to find you. Hold on, Baby."

"Mags, your voice is getting lower. I can hardly hear you. Hurry! Hurry!"

Panic manifested inside me as the clouds thickened and Annie's voice began to trail off. "I won't leave you Annie! I won't let you die alone!"

My deep gasp awakened me and it startled my husband, who came running into the room.

"Maggie, are you okay?"

I felt numb, recalling reality. "Yeah, okay as I can be. What time is it?"

"It's eleven-thirty."

"Oh my God! I slept that late?"

Greg sat on the bed and stroked my hair. "You had a hard day yesterday. You were out like a light just minutes after you took that Ambien. I called Don for you to let him know what's happened and he

KELLY O'CALLAN

called in a couple of prescription sedatives for you. He sends you his love and prayers."

"What about Mom and Ollie?" Did they get here yet?"

Greg dropped his head and sighed. "No, they haven't gotten here."

"It's late. I thought they might've been here by now."

Greg took one of my hands in his and looked solemnly into my eyes. His eyes began to fill with tears. "Maggie, I don't know how to tell you this... but..."

I filled with fear. "What?"

"Ollie called this morning. Your mom's in the hospital. She had some complications with her heart in the middle of the night."

I quickly made my way to the brightly lit reception area. "Hello. Could you please tell me the room number for Patricia Von Worth?"

"And you are?"

"Her daughter, Margaret. She was brought to the E. R. in the middle of the night with heart problems."

The receptionist's fingers danced quickly about the computer's keyboard. "Okay, Margaret. Your mother was transported here last night via ambulance with symptoms of shock and respiratory failure. She's currently in the I.C.U."

I dashed like a mad woman out of the elevator, leaving Greg several steps behind. I stood in the front desk area of the I.C.U. "My name is Margaret Simmons, and I'm here to see my mother, Patricia Von Worth."

The nurse led me, and only me, to my mother's room. She was permitted only two visitors at a time, so I assumed Ollie was the other person who was already in the room with her.

"Oh my dear, Maggie," Ollie greeted me, face wet from tears, and with open arms. "I'm so glad you made it here."

I hugged him with reserve, hastily wanting to assess what was

180

happening to my mother. Upon letting him go, I walked over to her bedside, and it appeared as though every medical machine created was hooked up to her tiny body.

I placed my hand on a bare spot on her arm and called out to her. "Mom. Mom. Can you hear me? It's Maggie."

"She's in a coma," Ollie tells me. "She can't respond to you."

I gulped. "What happened to her, Ollie?"

He shook his head. "If only she had seen that Sister Helena woman sooner. Maybe she would've gone ahead and scheduled for the pacemaker to be put in sooner. And she'd be okay now."

"What are you talking about?"

"When Sister Helena told your Mom she had a sick heart, that scared her enough to finally do something about it."

My eyes remained inquisitive.

Ollie sat down on a thick, padded chair and began rubbing the top of his thighs with his hands. "Maggie, I know your mother never told you about this, but she has progressive heart disease. She was diagnosed with it early last year, and I knew she never wanted you girls to know about it so I kept my mouth shut about it, too. Last night, when you told us about Annie, your Mom took the news pretty badly. Her body went into shock, and it was probably too much for her heart to take. She got really pale, and began sweating all over. Then she started vomiting, and eventually passed out. When I couldn't arouse her, I called an ambulance over right away. They hooked her up to a defibrillator, and were able to revive her. But, they don't know if her heart will ever be able to beat on its own again."

I looked down disbelievingly at my sleeping mother's placid face.

Ollie went on. "You see, the doctors said when the body goes into shock, it causes lack of blood flow to vital organs. And that can cause some massive damage to organs and tissue, leading to multiple organ failure, and possibly to death."

"Are you telling me that Mom is gonna die?"

"I don't know what's gonna happen," he whispered.

I heard a gentle knock on the door.

"Hello, there," said a tall red-haired man in his early fifties wearing a long white overcoat and a friendly smile. "How is everyone holding up?"

"Dr. Anson," started Ollie. "This here is Maggie. One of Pat's daughters. She came up from Philadelphia."

"Ah, yes. I have an aunt from Philadelphia," Dr. Anson said as he shook my hand. "How are you holding up today?"

"Not very well, Dr. Anson," I replied wearily.

He nodded. "Yes, I'm sorry to hear about the loss of your sister."

"Thank you."

"And now you have to deal with the situation here with your mother."

I choked on my voice. "Dr. Anson, what's going to happen to her?"

He rested his palms on Mom's bed rail and spoke matter-of-factly. "Well, Maggie, your mom went into shock, which caused ventricular fibrillation of the heart, and right now, we are in the process of trying to determine exactly how much damage has been done."

"What kind of damage?"

"Maggie, your mother's heart gave out on her. There is a pumping device inserted into her heart to keep it beating, a respirator hooked up to her to maintain her breathing, intravenous fusion to feed her, and dialysis to remove waste material."

"For how long?"

"Well, that depends."

"On what?"

"The results of her MRI and EEG."

"And what are those tests for?"

"Maggie, those tests are going to be run on your mother so we can find out if she may or may not be brain-dead."

I pressed my face onto the smooth window of the passenger door as my husband drove me home. I watched the world going on outside my window as the world inside of me was being destroyed. It broke my heart to leave my ill-fated mother's bedside, but I needed to return home to make funeral arrangements for Annie and to stop by Detective Colletti's office.

We arrived at Detective Colletti's office shortly after 4 p.m. He took Greg and I into a small room that was filled with volumes of papers scattered about, and closed the door.

"I'm glad you made it by, Maggie. I was just about to call you."

"Yeah? Well, I'm just getting back from a ride I had up to New York. My mother's in the hospital."

Detective Colletti's face soured. "Oh no. Sorry to hear that. Nothing serious, I hope."

Greg answered for me as I wiped a tissue underneath my sore eyes. "Unfortunately, it doesn't look good. It's her heart."

Colletti shook his head. "Tragedies. They always seem to happen in clusters. Anyhow, I got the report from the coroner's office regarding the cause and manner of Annie's death."

I sat upright. "What happened to her?"

He read from his report. "Cause of death... toxic lethal dosage of alcohol and barbituates. Manner of death... accidental, possible suicide."

"*What?*" I gasped. "That can't be. Annie doesn't take drugs. And she'd never kill herself. How can that be?"

Detective Colletti turned on the sympathy. "Look, Maggie, I'm truly sorry for your loss. Your sister had a little too much alcohol and Valium in her system which caused severe liver damage. Her system began shutting down on her. In the end, the poor girl ended up choking on her own poisonous vomit."

"You're wrong," I countered. "Somebody killed her. Somebody else did that to her. Annie was *NOT* a drug abuser!"

"Ms. Simmons, one of my men found both Valium and crystal meth along with some other amphetamines by her bedside table and in her bathroom cabinet. And there was no evidence indicating foul play."

"It was Mick! He killed her. Just like Alexis LeNoir. And other women, too!"

"Calm down, Maggie!" Greg urged me. "You're getting carried away."

"I have a copy of her death certificate here," Detective Colletti continued, "and her body is ready to be released from the morgue."

"Is that it?" I asked.

"Did we miss something?"

"That's it? You're not gonna investigate any further into Annie's death?"

Colletti sighed. "Maggie, I'm sorry. But everything's done here. You need to go ahead and make funeral arrangements for your sister. I know it was difficult to hear the contents of the autopsy report, thinking that maybe there was something you could've done to save her. But, apparently Annie had a dirty little secret. A dirty little secret that would sadly end up taking her life."

CHAPTER TWENTY-FOUR

The moment I was dreading for days had arrived much quicker than it should have. Until the moment I arrived at Keller's Funeral Home, I had been trying to come to terms with the reality of what happened in the most sane manner possible. I tried to make sense of it all and cope with the loss. Any self-calming success I managed to achieve in my mind was blown away when I saw Annie lying motionless in her coffin.

I arrived an hour earlier than her scheduled wake, so I could have some final private time of my own with her. I knelt down alongside her and marveled at how beautiful she looked. She wore the white satin dress that I had picked out for her upcoming thirtieth birthday, a milestone she would now miss by a mere sixteen days. Her hair was curled like fluffy ribbons around her angelic face and her lips were painted a delicate rose-petal pink.

An unexpected rush of anger grew inside me. I cursed God. It was wrong what had happened. I'd always dreamed that one day I'd be helping Annie to plan out her wedding and pick out a dress for that special day. But, instead, I had arranged for her burial. All the while, also dealing with the burden, in the back of my mind, of deciding if I should take my brain-dead mother off of life support or not. It was just too much to bear. I grabbed the bottle of Xanax from my purse and swallowed two capsules whole.

I touched Annie's cheek lightly, mortified at the feel of the hard, coldness of her skin. I shivered in response. "Hey, Annie. It's me. Your crazy big Sis. I miss you. You know that? Life is gonna be pretty hard for me without you around. It's gonna be real tough."

I began to weep. "I remember the day, when Mom sat me on her lap, and she whispered to me that she had a great surprise for me. She said, 'Margaret Anne, guess what? Mommy's gonna have a baby!' I was so excited. Mommy told me that you were gonna be my baby, too. And you know what, Annie? You were. You were my baby, too. And I loved you, more than just like a sister. More like the love a mother has for her child. And, I'm so, so sorry Mommy can't be here with you right now to say goodbye to you."

I pressed my fingers into the golden tresses that rested on top of the pillow. "I'll miss you so much, Sweetie. I wish you could come back. I wish you didn't have to die. There's so much more we were supposed to do together. You had your whole life ahead of you. It wasn't supposed to be like this. I'm so sorry for the hurt and pain I caused you, and I hope that you can forgive me. I'll make whoever did this to you pay. Do you hear me? I promise you. I promise you that."

An aberrant scowl quickly crossed my lips.

"Oh, my darling, oh, my darling,
Oh, my darling, Clementine,
You are lost and gone forever,
Dreadful sorry, Clementine.
You are lost and gone forever,
Dreadful sorry, Clementine."

Derek, who felt most comfortable staying with his Aunt Carol for the time being, knelt down quietly beside me. "She doesn't look real. She kinda looks weird... like she's a statue or something."

I wrapped my arm around my son. "I know. But she's still beautiful, isn't she?"

"Yeah," he agreed. "Aunt Annie always looked really pretty. Even a couple of my buddies at school had crushes on her."

I giggled softly in reminiscence. "Derek, your Aunt Annie used to have loads of boys that would walk her home back when she was in school. Your grandmom used to be so embarrassed. She would tell her, 'Annie Von Worth, you better cut the strings with some of those

186

fellows you're walking around with before the whole neighborhood goes thinking that my little girl is the town tramp.' Annie would just laugh at her and say, 'But Mom, it's not my fault! The more I ask them to leave me alone, the more they follow me around!'"

We shared a moment of silence before Derek's saddened eyes met with mine. "Mom, did you love Aunt Annie?"

I was stunned by his question. "Why, of course I did. Why on earth would you ask such a thing?"

He glanced back down at the aunt he loved so well. "I don't know. Like, that fight you had with her and all. Why did you cheat on Dad? And why with Aunt Annie's boyfriend? Were you mad at them both or something?"

The feeling in my previously gutted insides came back, filled with shame. "Honey, I don't know why I did the things I did. It was stupid, immature, and I messed up. There has not been a day that has gone by since that I haven't ask myself why I did what I did. Just know that, I love your Dad, and Aunt Annie, too, and that I've never meant to hurt anybody with what I've done."

Derek dropped his head on my shoulder and his voice quivered. "Why can't things be like they were before, Mom? Can't you and Dad at least get back together?"

I swallowed my son up in my arms. "I don't know what's gonna happen, Sweetheart. I just don't know. Dad was very hurt by what I did. Only time will tell what will happen between us."

My mood turned grimmer as people arrived and bid their condolences to me, and paid their respects to Annie. So much life was in the room, and none inside Annie's body. My inability to accept her death had left my mind playing games with me. I would find myself periodically looking over my shoulder into the casket, hoping I'd notice that she had moved, indicating that she was still alive. Sadly, she stayed motionless.

Aside from my mother, Derek and myself, Annie had no living

relatives. Many of the people that came to her viewing were co-workers, friends, and a few of her past lovers. Several members of Greg's family, including his parents, were there to offer me warmth and support. I graciously accepted their blessings and prayers for my sister, forcing a humble smile with each 'thank you' I gave. But, unfortunately, I couldn't find it in my heart to create a smile and a sincere thank you for her friend, Trista.

"I'm so sorry to hear about Annie, Maggie," she spoke sympathetically. "She was my best and dearest friend since high-school and I'm gonna miss her deeply."

"Oh, Trista, you don't fool me a bit," I unexpectedly snapped.

She looked startled. "Excuse me?"

I felt uninhibited, making my final case for poor Annie. "I said you don't fool me. You have quite the nerve to call her your best friend. You didn't include her in half the things that you did. You remained secretive about the whereabouts of a man she once loved, and Christ, you even ripped her out of being in your bridal party just months prior to the wedding! What kind of friend is that?"

Trista was shocked, and instantly moved to tears. "How can you say that about me? Do you wanna know why I didn't ask Annie out to some of the places that I went to? Because half the time she wouldn't show up, no call, nothing. So I stopped asking. And do you wanna know why I never told her about Sam and Dina? Because they were very happy together, and Sam didn't have to deal with Annie's unpredictability anymore."

She wiped her face with a crumpled tissue. "And as far as my wedding goes, it was one of the hardest decisions I've had to make in my life, deciding if I wanted her in it or not. You have no idea how many nights I lost sleep over making the decision to have Natalie take Annie's place as my maid-of-honor. But, it all boiled down to knowing that Natalie would show up. And on time. Without being drunk or hung over."

"Why are you talking about Annie like that?"

Trista sniffled and her eyes grew saucer-like. "Oh, my God. You still don't know, do you?"

"Know what?"

Trista's face was plastered with genuine guilt and I could tell she felt uneasy about saying what she was about to say. "Maggie, your sister was an alcoholic."

"Annie? No, that's not true. You must be confused. Why would you say a thing like that?"

By the sincere look on her face, I could tell that she wasn't confused at all. "She never wanted you to know, Maggie. She loved you so much and looked up to you, and didn't want to disappoint you. She knew if you ever found out, it would crush you. She tried her best to keep it a secret. She tried to keep it a secret from me for years, until one day she swallowed her pride and broke down to tell me. But, she made me swear to keep quiet about it. And I did. Because I loved her. And I still do."

Every existing cell in my body became numb.

Trista placed her hand on my elbow. "I'm so sorry I had to be the one to tell you, Maggie. I just wished Annie had gotten herself some help. Then none of us would have to be here saying goodbye to her today."

I rushed into the bathroom and splashed some cold water onto my face. I wished that Mom was here with me. I suddenly felt so alone in what I was going through and craved my mother's strength and presence to comfort me. I took a few deep breaths and coached myself to be strong upon my exiting of the restroom.

"Maggie?" I heard a man's voice say behind me.

I turned around to find a nice-looking, impeccably dressed African-American man staring at my face inquisitively. He then bore a righteous smile. "Yeah, that's the face of the other little girl in the painting."

I placed a hand over my mouth. "Charles?"

His grin grew brighter. "Yes! That's me. I worked with your sister,

Annie."

Some unknown force caused me to walk forward and give that man a hug. "Charles, thank you for being here. Annie talked so much about you. She would've been so grateful you came here today."

He wiped a fresh tear that glistened in his eye. "Annie spoke a lot about you, too. She said you loved the painting I made of the two of you at the mountains when you were little girls."

I nodded. "Yes, I really love that painting. And it will mean more to me now than I ever imagined it could. Thank you."

Charles' pure-hearted smile gradually drifted off his face. "I just... I just don't understand what's happened here. I just don't know how Annie died the way she did. I thought I talked things through with her. But, I guess it didn't work."

"You mean, her drinking?" I asked.

"No, I mean what happened between her and Mick and all. She was completely distraught over it. I noticed right away something was wrong with her. She didn't want to talk to me about it. And that wasn't like her. She always told me everything."

"I know she confided in you a lot, Charles," I responded. "I think she really trusted you. And I don't think she felt she had many people she could trust in her life."

"I know," he spoke with dark, forthright eyes, "she told me repeatedly in these last couple of months that, besides her mother, I was all she had. I know she took the loss of both you and Mick in her life pretty hard. She really fell hard for Mick. I never seen her so totally destroyed by a break-up before. But, the part I don't understand is, them saying she died with drugs in her body. I knew Annie, inside and out. And I know that Annie would have never, ever touched any bad stuff. Never."

"I know," I agreed, drawing a deep breath. "I'm just having a difficult time grasping the fact that she was an alcoholic, too."

Charles shook his head. "I knew all about her problem with binge drinking. I've known it for years. Like I told you, she would tell me everything. And I know for a fact, Annie wouldn't dare touch any of them drugs or shit like they say she did."

"Maybe she did," I reasoned. "Maybe she did take it, in fact, to commit suicide."

Charles raised his hands to his side. "But, why? What would she have done that for?"

"I don't know. Maybe because of how devastated she felt by what Mick and I had done. And mostly, like you said, because of the devastation she felt by losing the man she fell head-over-heels for."

"You see, that's the part that don't make sense to me. Because just a couple of weeks ago, Annie and Mick had gotten back together."

"Wait. Did you just say that Annie and Mick had gotten back together?"

"Yeah, she told me that they had went and patched things up together. Just that, they had to keep it quiet for awhile. She never really told me why."

Annie's memorial service was beautiful, and Derek read a touching tribute to 'his favorite aunt' at the podium. I was proud of him. He held his composure up well as he voiced his personal eulogy to her, leaving not one dry eye left in the church.

It was just after noontime when we made it to the cemetery. Annie was to be buried in one of the six plots Mom had purchased years ago, alongside of Dad. The officiating priest had given his final prayer of peace, and then invited all to lay a rose on top of Annie's coffin. Staring at the fresh pile of dirt that was soon to be placed on top of Annie, this final moment of goodbye seemed the hardest for me. I watched as each person, who was an intricate part of Annie's life, placed their final gesture of love, in the form of a pink rose, atop of her permanent wooden bed. To prevent myself from drowning in grief, I clutched firmly onto Greg and Derek for strength to cope with my loss. But suddenly, my bleak moment of sorrow became clouded by wrath when I noticed Mick Dillon standing inconspicuously along some fresh budding trees in the distance.

KELLY O'CALLAN

CHAPTER TWENTY-FIVE

Feverish emotions ran amuck in my mind after I returned from Annie's burial. I sprinted into my bedroom, pulling open dresser drawers and thrashing clothes about in my closet, looking for something comfortable to wear to go see Mom. Adding to my heartache, was the disappointment I felt in Derek, who didn't want to ride up with me to see his grandmother because he felt he'd be too uncomfortable seeing her hooked up to the machines. He went back to stay with his Aunt Carol, while Greg and I planned on taking the trip to the hospital together.

"Maggie, are you okay?" Greg asked, his voice bathed in worry, as I fumbled through my pile of clothing.

I stared back at him, exhausted, falling onto the bed.

He sat beside me, raised his hand gently to my cheek, and caressed it. I leaned my head onto his shoulder and placed his other hand securely into mine. I closed my ache-swollen eyes. We spoke no words and all that could be heard between us was the synchronizing sound of our breaths. Soon, we started kissing.

We found shelter from the cloud of death from the life force that beat within us. It was the first time Greg and I had been intimate since 'the incident' took place. I felt so comforted in feeling the warmth, the touch, the taste, and the scent of my husband's skin. I made love to him with great need, feeling the same passionate intensity that blazed within him in return.

Afterward, we lay quietly; my head resting upon his furry chest. I listened appreciatively to the sound of his beating heart. It was

193

something I missed desperately for months.

"Greg, I've missed you so much," I moaned. "I'm so glad you're back now and we can be a family again."

I felt his body stiffen as he searched for a response. "Maggie, under the circumstances, I felt that it was good for me to be here with you to help get you through this difficult time you're dealing with. But... I never said to you that I was going to be coming back home."

"You're not?" I cried.

Greg took a deep sigh. "Maggie, I'm sorry. But, I never told you I was coming back."

I pulled myself away from him. "What? I don't understand. Don't you think you've punished me enough already?"

"*Punished you?*" Greg's voice flared. "You think my leaving you was for a means of *punishing* you? Maggie, you cheated on me with another man! You broke a huge commitment of trust we shared together! And you know me well enough to know that's not something I take lightly."

"Yes, I know what I did. And I've told you I'm sorry! What more do you want from me?"

"I need to know that it will never happen again."

"It won't ever happen again. I promise, I swear!"

Greg looked uneasy. "How could I ever be sure, Maggie? You broke your marriage vows to me once. How could I possibly be sure you wouldn't do it again?"

A wave of sickness wallowed up inside me. "Get out."

Greg's eyes widened. "What did you just say?"

I crawled out of bed and onto my feet, clutching the sheet. "I said get out!"

He was stunned to silence.

"Go leave then, if you don't wanna be with me. I don't need your goddamn pity."

"Now, calm down, Maggie. Let's be real here. You need me here right now."

"What for?" I growled. "So you can constantly throw in my face what I've done to you? You'd love to hang that one over my head, wouldn't you? You'd use my episode of unfaithfulness as a reference point for any wrong thing I'd do in the future, wouldn't you, Greg?"

Greg placed his hands, palms facing forward, in front of him. "Now hold on, Maggie. We have bigger issues to worry about now, like getting up to see your mother. We can talk about what's going on with us later, at a more appropriate time."

I drew in a deep, congested breath. "No, Greg. You see, that's the problem. There never WAS an appropriate time that you would agree to talk about us in the past. You always put anything that had to do with our marriage last on your list. It only goes to show me where I truly was on your priority list. At the bottom, I guess. So, you're probably right to assume you couldn't trust me to seek comfort in the arms of another man again. After all, in the end it was your lack of interest in me that caused me to turn there in the first place."

The drive up to New York to see Mom was very painful. Much of the journey, which I'd taken alone, has been blurred from my memory. All I remember were the wretched, convoluted thoughts that ebbed and flowed in my mind concerning Annie, Mom, and my irrational outburst with Greg. I thought for sure I'd have gotten killed in a nasty car wreck as I drove inattentively on the New Jersey Turnpike. Although it didn't happen, I don't think I would have cared if it did.

"We just left a message on your machine about an hour ago," the reception area nurse told me. "Your mother is not doing well. I'll page Dr. Anson to come in and speak with you."

The lighting was low inside Mom's room and it crushed me inside to see her lying helplessly on her future deathbed, hooked up to all sorts of machinery that would end up recording the final beat of her failing heart.

"I'm sorry to tell you this," spoke Dr. Anson. "But your mother's vital organs are starting to shut down completely. We've witnessed both kidney and liver failures occur within the last couple of hours."

My eyes burned and my voice trembled. "How long, Dr. Anson?"

His eyes held onto gloom. "Seventy-two hours. I'm so sorry, Maggie."

I sat down beside my mother and held her delicate hand.

She died later that night.

CHAPTER TWENTY-SIX

In the days and weeks after Mom's death, my life consisted of pill popping and abstract thinking. Being awake was dreadful, and trying to sleep was a nightmare. The sky was a dismal dark gray in that rainy month of April, 2000, as was the mood inside my distraught head.

Aside from visits with Derek, which were growing more and more infrequent, I just about lost all contact I had with the outside world, keeping confined to the inside walls of my bedroom. Alone in my bed, I cried many tears of sorrow, trying to make sense of it all... life, death, and the paradoxes that lie between them.

I grieved heavily over the losses in my life, desperately trying to figure out how everything tragically got to this point. How did I go from being Margaret Simmons 'the success story' to Margaret Simmons 'the cataclysmic story'? Where did I go wrong? Was it something I did? Was it the result of someone else's doing? Or was it simply God's hand that controlled everything as fate would have it?

Unhealthy thoughts ran rampantly inside my drug-induced, warped mind causing the clear likelihood of my falling victim to delusions fueled by my guilt and sorrow. Simply put, I felt I was on the verge of suffering a nervous breakdown. It was either that or I'd have to willingly surrender to the pleasures and pitfalls of becoming a drug addict. I needed to choose my form of escape before fate chose it for me.

Luckily, on just the day I thought I was about to totally lose my mind, I got a phone call. It was Annie's landlord. He reminded me that all her belongings needed to be cleared out by the end of the week or it was all was going in the trash. This was a task I was dreading, mainly for sentimental reasons. But, alas, it needed to be done, and I needed a reason to be forced out of bed.

It was quite difficult to step into Annie's vacant home. Things were left as they were the last day I'd been there, with the police taping and markings still in the bedroom. There was even a faint whiff of the ghastly stench of death and bleach that lingered in the air. I opened the windows, letting in some fresh air and spray from raindrops.

I felt it best to keep my mind focused on the task at hand by just putting all her belongings into several large trash bags and storing them in my attic. I'd sort through them at a later time. I decided to start with her clothes closet.

When my eyes first caught glimpse of the familiar apparel, that overwhelming sense of sentiment I feared washed over me. I grabbed onto a few of her shirts and dresses, squeezing them and holding them up to my nose to smell any trace of her scent. I dropped to the floor, garments in hand, and just let the tears flow.

From that point on, I moved quickly, packing her jewelry, pictures, books, music cd's, and other belongings with numbed emotion. It wasn't until I made it into the kitchen that I came across something peculiar.

As I was packing up her mugs and glasses, I came across the small recorder I had given her back in October. It was obviously placed in a spot where it would be hidden, behind a tall, dark glass in the back of the cupboard. I took the recorder with me into the living room, where I sat on the couch.

I rewound some of the tape and pressed play.

I first heard Annie's voice.

"Mick, I can't believe you went out and bought my sister a nice gift like that! How did you get the money to pay for a necklace like that when you needed to borrow three-hundred dollars from me just weeks

ago? Is that what you needed the money for?"

"No, baby, I told you I needed that money to pay off a gambling debt I had. And I did. Don't worry. I'll get that money back to you as soon as I get it. Something really big is coming to me soon. A real big payoff. Just be patient with me. My ace is on the way."

I sat in disbelief as I listened in on various conversations that Annie had with Mick. I listened to Annie bear her frustrations over her problems with alcohol to him, as he spoke of his own difficulties with gambling and drug addiction. At one point on the recording, I heard Mick persistently try to persuade Annie into sharing a line of meth with him. She repeatedly refused his offer. I was enraged.

But, nothing angered me as much as what I heard at the end of the tape.

"I don't understand!" Annie cried out. *"Why do you have to keep us a secret right now? Why can't I come and see you at work tonight? Are you ashamed of me?"*

Mick's voice was insistent. *"Please, Annie. Just for a little while longer. It's just not safe yet. I need to make sure all my cards are in place before I settle my game. I want to make sure, in the end, that I am a winner. That I am the cardholder."*

"What are you talking about, Mick? What is this metaphor with the cards and a game you keep talking about?"

With that, I heard a door slam and the tape's recordings end.

I drove my car at the highest speed I've ever driven, ran into the

Police Department building, and dropped the recorder onto Detective Colletti's desk.

"I want you to re-open the investigation on the death of my sister now!"

Detective Colletti seemed displeased with my abrupt intrusion. "What's going on here?"

I pointed to the recorder. "I have evidence on that tape that Annie's boyfriend, Mick Dillon, was the one who did the drugs and that she, in fact, didn't. Also, that they were having problems in their relationship around the time that she died."

Colletti grabbed his face. "Ms. Simmons... I don't know what more it is that I can say to you. You need to put to come to terms with the fact that your sister died by means of drug and alcohol toxicity by her own doing. If her intentions were purposeful or accidental, that cannot be proven by means of speculation. *No one* killed your sister, Maggie."

"But, on these tapes, you'll hear how Mick was doing drugs and that Annie was never interested in taking any herself. That's got to prove something."

Colletti shook his head in disgust. "Annie's prints, and *only* Annie's prints were found on all the drug paraphernalia and on the bottle of whiskey she drank that was found at the side of her bed."

"What about the man that the neighbor said she saw come in with Annie that night?"

"The man checked out fine. He was just a fellow at the bar where she was who offered her a ride home when he noticed how drunk she was that night. We questioned him, and he claims he just drove her home, got her inside, and left. He told us she made a pass at him to have sex, but he declined. All the evidence confirms that his story is true."

"Which bar was it?"

"The lounge at the Mason Pierce Hotel."

"That's where Mick Dillon works! Don't you guys get it?"

Detective Colletti looked at me with pity in his eyes. "Maggie, you need to stop with the over-analyzing things and put your ridiculous theories to rest. It's not good to think about things too much. You could easily drive yourself crazy. If you want, I have the number of an excellent grief counselor should you need it."

When I arrived home to the prison walls of my bedroom, I couldn't seem to stop the manic circus that was going on in my head. My bottle of Valium sat poised on top of my dresser, sneakily disguised as a remedy, calling out my name. I was angry over what becoming of me. I grabbed the pills and threw them towards the mirror, causing a spider web-like crack in the center.

I began hyperventilating and breaking out into a cold sweat. I refused to be a casualty of my pain. I needed immediate relief. I needed... answers.

It was a Friday evening, so I thought it would be a good idea for me to take a ride over to the M.P. Lounge. When I arrived, around 10 p.m., there seemed to be a big party going on. The lounge was filled with balloons, streamers, and banners that read "GOOD LUCK." I scanned the room for Mick, but didn't see him. I then walked slowly towards the bar, in hopes of spotting Sara.

"Can I help you?" asked a barmaid.

I forced a smile. "Yes, can you tell me if Mick is here tonight?"

The woman gave me a gracious frown. "Oh, I'm sorry. You just missed him by like a couple minutes. He left already."

"Okay, how about Sara?" Is she here tonight?"

"No, Sara doesn't work here anymore. She left a couple of weeks ago."

"Maybe you could help me," I said pulling out a photo of Annie and showing it to her. "Do you recognize this woman?"

The barmaid's face turned expressionless. "Yeah, her name's Annie, right?"

I felt a glimmer of hope. "You know her?"

"Yeah," she answered, her eyes filling with pity just as Coletti's did earlier. "She's the girl who died last month. I was working the last night she was in here."

"Oh, please, can you tell me anything you remember about that night?"

She looked uneasy, calculating her recollection. "Well, there's not much I can tell you, except, she seemed really upset. And very drunk."

"Was she here by herself?"

"I'm not sure. She was sitting mostly at the bar, I remember, and I think Sara was still here, and she waited on her mostly."

"Was Mick here that night?"

"Yeah, it looked as if Annie wanted to talk to him, but he kinda ignored her and stuff. She was really drawing a lot of attention to herself. I remembered her being really loud. Finally, I think Sara asked one of our regulars, Dave, to escort her out and make sure she got home okay."

Sara. I needed to talk to Sara.

"Do you have Sara's phone number?"

"Sorry, I don't."

"And what about Mick? When is he due in next?"

Her eyebrow vexed in confusion. "Mick won't be back in."

"Why not?" I asked.

"Well, today was his last day," she explained. "We just wrapped up the going away party we had for him. He's moving to Chicago. His plane leaves tomorrow morning."

CHAPTER TWENTY-SEVEN

It was during the drive home from the M.P. Lounge when I first felt the throes of the death trance. Its evil grasp took hold of me quickly, without warning, and it fed hungrily upon the overwhelming fury in my blood.

I was outraged at God, at Mick, at myself, and the world. Life seemed to be nothing more than a perverse joke.

Or was it?

Maybe it was, as Mick had repeatedly put it, like a game. And if life was, in fact, a game, I sure as hell wasn't going to be holding the losing hand. And in order for me to be a winner, someone else had to be a loser.

As the morbid trance feasted heavily upon me, the desire to end my life, and my pain, grew stronger. Suicide would be such an easy way out from the unbearable pain. I had nothing to lose that I hadn't lost already. My life, as I knew it, was over.

I walked with weighted heels into my bedroom and searched for the box that sat on the closet shelf. I pulled out the Smith and Wesson .38, and stared at it. I carefully placed two bullets in the carriage and contemplated my final game strategy in life.

If I choose to live in my ill-fated world, God wins and I lose.

If I choose to die by my own hand, God loses, and so do I. Nobody wins.

There had to be a better way to do this, I thought. I wanted a situation where I would win, and God lost. I was angry at Him for taking my life from me and wanted Him to pay. I wanted to take away His role as the Dealer, having control over fate.

Maybe I couldn't take control of my own fate, but I certainly could have power over someone else's.

But, was it He that took my life from me? Or, was someone else playing my life cards, without my knowing it? Stealing my Ace? Like Alexis LeNoir had hers stolen from her? Like Annie's had been taken from her? Jen Harris' too? How long was the list?

The solution to my dilemma was easy to see. The problem was with the scoundrel that came into my life, and threw it upside down. The reasons why I did not yet understand, but I tried to piece things together in my head.

I recalled my visit with Sister Helena with Mom and Annie. She told Mom she had a sick heart. She told Annie the water she drank from was poisonous. She told me to use my wisdom in my darkest hour.

My darkest hour was here. And although my wisdom might result in sacrificing myself, I knew that I had to save all the other Jen Harris', Alexis LeNoirs, and Annie Von Worths of the world from becoming victims to Mick's game playing. I put my wisdom to work in finally figuring out Mick Dillon, and his game, once and for all.

My state of emotion fluctuated between raw and numb on the fateful drive I took to Mick's apartment that dark, windy Friday night. The game plan was etched in my head and I knew how to win. There was simply no stopping it.

He was surprised to see me when he opened the door. "Maggie? It's late. What are you doing here?"

I could tell by the sound of his voice that he was nervous. "Would you mind if I came in? There's a little something I'd like to talk you about."

204

"Ah... this really isn't a good time. Maybe you could come by tomorrow afternoon and we could talk better then."

"I thought your flight was leaving first thing in the morning?" I asked with a cold voice.

He sighed, and reluctantly opened his door to me.

"Would you care for something to drink? I really don't have much left besides water and a couple of beers."

"No, that's okay," I answered, scanning the partially emptied room. "I don't plan on staying long."

"Don't mind me, I have a little last minute packing to do," he spoke, purposely averting his eyes from meeting mine. "What is it that you wanted to talk to me about?"

"Why haven't you returned any of my phone calls?" I said, studying his face, noticing his much lighter hair-color.

"I don't think it would've been a good idea, given the circumstances," he replied, heading towards his bedroom. "You know that there could've been nothing more between us after that day."

I followed him into the bedroom. I wanted to see his face. "Why did you tell Annie about what happened between you and me?"

"I didn't," he answered carefully, sensing my iciness, "She found your earring on the bed and figured it all out by herself."

"You're lying," I snapped through gritted teeth. "Just like you lied when you said Jill Coopersmith recommended you to me. You've never even exchanged words with the woman!"

It was then that I pulled out the gun from my jacket and pointed it at him.

Mick's eyes blinked with incredulity. "Maggie, what are you *doing*?"

I took a deep breath. "I'm playing your game, Mick."

He stood in place like a statue. "Please, Maggie. Put that thing down. What game are you talking about?"

I raised my eyebrow in a questioning slant. "Oh, come now, Mick. I thought you'd know better than that! You're the gambler here! You know, the game of life. The card game of life."

"I don't know what you're talking about," he spoke, gasping, with eyes widened in alarm.

I walked forward; he backed himself to the wall.

I spoke calmly, fluidly, toying with him. "Mick, you disappoint me. Don't you remember in my office? The sessions we had? The talks about being the cardholder?"

He remained rigid with terror.

"You know," I continued, "about how to get that winning hand in life? About how to get that Ace. You know what I'm talking about."

His voice degenerated to a childlike whimper. "Look, please Maggie. It's not what you think."

"*Who do you think you're talking to?* I know how you play your game! You like that feeling you get when you win at something, don't you? You love the high you get when you've won a woman's heart, don't you? It feels just like winning the jackpot at the casino, doesn't it? You're addicted to that high, and you'll let nothing stand in your way, even if it means breaking innocent women's hearts along the way, isn't that right?"

"No, you've got everything wrong, Dr. Simmons. Please, let me explain."

"You don't have to explain a thing to me," I said, lips curled in disgust. "The reason you came to me was to get that Ace in your hand. And that Ace, for you, was in being able to make women fall blindly in love with you, so you could get anything you wanted out of them. Especially their money. And you used me. You used me as your guinea pig to test out your phony love trance. And I fell for it. Just like Alexis did. Just like Annie did. And just like Jen Harris and whoever else there was did."

"Wait! Who's Jen Harris?" he asked, eyes widening innocently.

"*Shut up!*" I growled with rage. "You ruined my life. I have lost EVERYTHING because of you. And I won't let you do it to anyone else."

He shook nervously, staring at the gun. "Please, don't shoot me, Maggie. I'm afraid. I don't wanna die! I can explain everything."

My ears didn't want to hear what his mouth had to say. "I have to shoot you, Mick. It's the only way I can take back my Ace from you. You took my life from me. Now, it's my turn to take your life from you."

My eyes brimmed with tears as I pulled the trigger. The sound was quick and deafening. Mick was hit in the chest and fell instantly upon impact.

"I win, Mick. You lose. Who's the cardholder now?"

He gave out a guttural scream as he writhed and convulsed in agony on the hardwood floor. He cried out to me, coughing and gasping for air. His face was dark with fear and blood poured freely from his contorted body. Within seconds, his wailing was forever silenced by death.

I remember I was sitting and rocking myself on the floor of Mick's bedroom when the cops arrived.

Detective Colletti rushed into the room, his face covered by a deepening hue of shame. "Oh, no. Maggie Simmons..."

CHAPTER TWENTY-EIGHT

It took almost a year before my case went to trial. In the end, I was convicted of first-degree murder by reason of insanity, thanks to Detective Colletti's testimony, and ordered to serve twenty years in prison with no chance of parole until my seventh year.

In the months before my trial, I was placed in an institution for the mentally ill. After several 'modern day' shock treatments and much time spent in solitary confinement, which is all a blur to me now, I'd been able to think a little clearly again. I began to wonder about myself, and the events that led up to my being capable of killing a man.

He was a man who was identified by the name of Michael Donovan, and whose true age was twenty-eight. It seemed that Michael Donovan, a.k.a. Mickey Dillon, actually went by several aliases, as he was a wanted man in many states with charges ranging from petty theft to numerous unpaid traffic violations. A man, whose face I see in my mind, and in my nightmares, every day.

There hadn't been a moment during the nights I spent in my 8' by 10' cell that I hadn't questioned my reasons for being there. I felt intense guilt for taking the life of another and the price I chose to pay was extremely high. My biggest punishment was sacrificing having a normal relationship with my son and watching him grow into a man. Missing out on being there with him when he graduates from school, gets married, or becomes a father for the first time. All I had to look forward to each waking morning was knowing that I was one day closer to my parole meeting, which was years away.

Life in prison is ugly. You have strict daily routines to follow and you have to deal with the fact that life is going on outside in the world and you can't be a part of it. The women in the facility are tough, too. You have to keep your means and wits about you at all times and be sure to never get on the bad side of a bully. I had been singled out by a couple of hard broads, who refer to me as 'pretty girl,' and I pray endlessly that I will never be subjected to a confrontation with any of them. I learned quickly it was best to keep to myself.

So, I sat mostly alone with my thoughts, wondering about the same thing over and over again in my head.

How did my life end up like this?

One day, I got my answer from a strange and unexpected visitor.

"You have a visitor 1289 (my prison ID#). Heather Jarvis. Time allotted is thirty minutes."

The name didn't ring a bell, and I thought it may have been some kind of mistake, but I sat and waited at the desk behind the plexiglass window. An attractive woman, close to my age, sat on the opposite side of the window. I thought she looked vaguely familiar to me. We lifted our phones.

"Well, hello there, Maggie," she spoke with a Londoner's accent, and in a condescending tone.

I narrowed my eyes, and peered closely at the woman. "Do I know you?"

She laughed mischievously and widened her eyes. "Oh, please, con't look that diff'rent without me specs on, can I?"

I gaped. "Sara, is that you?"

"Well, my name is really Heather. I buried that little mousy Sara out of my life, along with those bloody ugly glosses, and silly American accent long ago."

"Who are you?" I asked, confused.

Her lips pursed as she whispered. "Maggie, I'm your worst nightmare."

The blue in her eyes brightened with intensity and I instinctively knew that the purpose of her visit was to inflict harm.

"I want to make you suffer for what you did. And, I know, nothing could possibly hurt you more than the truth will."

I was becoming perturbed. "What are you talking about?"

Her eyes became serene. "It was a simple plan, really. Until you had to go and bring your sister into the picture."

"Who are you and what do you want?"

Heather giggled, exhibiting no shame. "You really don't know who I am, do you? Maybe this will ring a bell."

She poised herself upright. "Hello, J.T. Morgan and Associates. This is Heather speaking, to which extension would you like to be connected?"

She searched frenetically into my eyes for a response, finding perverse pleasure in what she found. "That's right, Maggie. I worked with your husband. And do you know how long and how well we've been working together? Five years. I've been fucking your husband now for five years."

I let out a voiceless scream as shock began to settle in.

"You look a little pale on the other side there," Heather said tapping on the window. "What's the matter? Cat's got your tongue?"

I swallowed dryly. "What plan are you talking about?"

"Ah, yes... the plan," she smiled pleasurably. "It was an *ingenius* idea, if I do say so myself. Let's start with the problem, shall we? Well, now you know Greg and I have been shagging for several years, but what you also didn't know was that along with being good in bed together, we made excellent embezzlement partners. We single-handedly had Carlson running to sign his resignation papers, when a colleague walked in on us doing something nasty. Carlson's abrupt departure provided Greg the perfect opportunity to advance to managerial status. I loved Greg, and wanted him all to myself. He told me that he'd never leave you without being able to take his son along with him. He felt it would be better to part ways with you when your son was of an appropriate age to be left home alone. He also needed to finagle his way out of your boring marriage with an excuse that would make Derek see him as the victim. That way, if things got to the point of having to go to court, the judge's decision to grant custody would easily go in Greg's favor. That is where Mick came into play."

I was ready to break through the plexiglass and strangle the bitch with my phone cord, but needed to keep my cool for behavioral purposes.

"The plan was," she went on, "in two parts, actually. Mick, an excellent con-artist, was to persuade Alexis LeNoir into investing large chunks of her inheritance money in our company, where Greg set up a phony account for her. I had left J.T. Morgan before the plan was put into effect, so Greg and I would not be connected to any wrongdoing. I got the job at the M.P. Lounge, a notable place where the big wigs hung out, to search out future money prospects for our scheming. That is where I actually met Mick, and it didn't take me long to figure out the potential he had to be a good bamboozler. I was actually the one who found Alexis for Mick, when Greg tipped me off to the fact that she would be attending a function for some animal charity at the hotel."

She bore an evil grin. "So, part one of the plan was successfully completed when Mick managed to get close to three million dollars out of Ms. LeNoir. Greg, Mick, and I were going to split the funds evenly. After, of course... Alexis' tragic death would occur."

"You sick bitch!" I spat in a whisper. "I knew Mick killed that woman!"

Heather shook her head. "But, no, Maggie. You're wrong. Mick was never able to do anything of that caliber. He was too sweet of a man to be able to kill anybody. He couldn't hurt a fly. Greg and I had charge of taking care of Alexis. But, Mick did have to do some more work to enable him to earn his fair share of the money. Money he needed desperately to help pay his crippled mother's medical bills in Florida, as well as his cancer-stricken brother's medical bills in Chicago. And some of his own gambling debts, of course."

I saw a quick image of the crippled woman somewhere in Florida who mourned with great ache for the son I had killed. I felt terrible for her.

"What did Mick have to do to get the money?" I asked straight-faced.

She leaned in close, searching into my eyes again for a response to what she was about to say. "He was to seduce you into having an affair with him. Make you cheat on your husband. That way, Greg would be easily able to leave your marriage, with all the fault being placed on you."

My eyes were seething and my voice grew bitter. "I don't believe you. I don't believe a word you just said. Why should I?"

Heather's eyebrows met and she continued taunting me. "You don't believe me so far? Okay, how about believing this! Mick's job was to make you have an affair so Greg would be able to leave the relationship innocently. They needed a solid plan, because Greg stressed that it would be hard for you, being a marriage therapist, to even think about breaking your own vows. That's when Mick thought about becoming one of your patients, giving him the opportunity to grow on you. And with the help of Greg, he would be able to penetrate into your mind and find a loophole in your way of thinking. Greg said your ego, when it came to your work, was huge. And you enjoyed the excessive stimulation with your work matters. So, Mick did just that."

"Meanwhile, Greg busied himself by becoming extra close to your son. He made sure he went to all his soccer games, took him to the amusement park when you weren't able to go, and even got the boy that dog to tighten their bond even further."

My throat tightened and a tear ran down my cheek. Heather didn't seem to notice and kept rambling on.

"Greg even purchased your blue sapphire diamond earrings as part of the plan, stressing that they be one-of-a-kind, so when Mick slipped it off of your ear when the sexual romp finally took place, you couldn't deny the fact that the earring was yours. Greg wanted you to wear those earrings everyday, not knowing for sure when the affair would take place. Mick did his part in getting you to wear the earrings by stressing the fact that he liked it when you wore blue. 'It's my favorite color', he'd tell you. To further insure you'd wear the earrings, he even went out and bought you a necklace to match."

My throat tightened even more, and I felt like I was being choked.

"But, you were a toughie, Maggie. You would not cheat on your husband easily. And then there was the problem that you sneakily brought your sister into the picture. Greg tipped off Mick as soon as you told him about your brilliant tape-recording idea, but it caused some complications. You needed a little more pushing, so that's what we did. I'd had the opportunity to speak to you that one night outside of the hotel. I fed into your ego by telling you that you needed to do anything and everything in your power to help Mick to learn about falling in love. Ha ha. I even threw in some rubbish about a girl named Jen Harris who supposedly killed herself over him."

I blinked. "Was that true? About that Jen Harris girl?"

Heather mocked me. "No! You fool! I made it up. But you went for it. You felt even more pressure to do your job well, didn't you? And Greg gave you some added pressure with the bet he made at your sister's friend's wedding. To make Mick be able to say 'I love you' before Valentine's Day. He said you hated losing bets to him, so he was sure you'd try everything in your power to beat him."

The familiar scenarios were coming back to me. I was stunned and speechless.

"And poor, Mick. He really loved your sister. He wanted desperately for he and Annie to be together and tried to get out of sleeping with you. He didn't want to jeopardize the relationship he had with Annie. Plus, I think he even genuinely liked and cared about you. But, he was in too deep and couldn't back out. He was terrified when he arrived at your office the day you told him it was to be his last session. He knew his time to persuade you to sleep with him was running out. Luckily, the weather had been bad that day, and he was able to convince you to go home with him. And, after he successfully slipped some amphetamines into your hot tea, leaving you feeling totally high and uninhibited, he knew he'd be able to complete his task."

She smiled in reminiscence. "The plan was complete."

I shook my head, "What about Annie? What happened to Annie at the bar the night she died at the bar?"

Heather's heavily made-up eyes turned sinister. "I knew Mick was still seeing her, which was not a smart move on his part. He repeatedly denied it to me. But, I had a feeling. Annie came into the bar that night to see him, and he made it seem to me that he was no longer dating her. But, she confided everything to me that evening. She thought I was her *new friend*. I just kept pouring the booze, dropping in a little pill here and a little pill there..."

I could hold my rage no longer. I rose like an explosive rocket from my chair, screaming at the top of my lungs and pounding ferociously on the plexi-glass. *"YOU BITCH! I'LL KILL YOU WHEN I GET OUT OF HERE! I'LL KILL YOU!!"*

The guard ran over quickly and tackled me to the chair. "You better cool your engines, 1289. Or it's solitary confinement for you."

I breathed heavily, composing myself. "Keep talking, Heather. I could turn you into the police, you know."

She rose her index finger and swung it back and forth. "No, no, now, Maggie, you wouldn't do a thing like that. That would mean that your husband would have to go to jail too, and then what would become of Derek? No parents? Well, he could always live with Greg's family, I suppose. You know, the family you were always jealous of Greg having, since you really didn't have one yourself."

I spit on the window.

Heather grimaced. "Maggie, such poor manners. You really should be on your best behavior or they might want to go ahead and delay your parole."

I burned inside. "Why are you here? Why are you telling me all of this?"

Heather's eyes returned to their earlier serene state. "I was there. I was there in the room that night when you shot Mick. I was hidden in the closet. He and I were getting ready to head off to Chicago the next morning. I was going to leave Greg, although he was unaware of it. He bitched and complained to me for years how hard it was living with you, how you analyzed every little thing in your relationship. Yet, when Annie and your mother died, he couldn't stand the guilt that haunted him because he left you. It was quite pathetic. He got on my bloody nerves."

"I still don't understand why you're telling me all of this now. What's your motive? What are you getting out of it?"

"It's quite simple, Maggie. It's all part of the game of life. You know, the game you played with Mick that evening in his bedroom. You didn't know it at the time, but there was another player involved. *ME.* You stole my Ace from me when you killed Mick. And now it's my turn to get my Ace back, and the Ace in my hand lies in the satisfaction of knowing that you now know what you've lost as a result of your actions and the true game that was played on you. If you had never gotten Annie involved, she and your mother would probably be alive today. If Mick and I had left for Chicago that next morning, Greg certainly would have returned to you with some extra big bucks in the bank and your life would have turned out fine. But, you played the wrong cards, Maggie, and you lost. I'm just here now, to let you know that, YOU are the loser and I'M the winner. That I am, in fact, the true cardholder. I was the dealer from the start. And always have been."

Days after Heather's revelatory visit, I found it difficult to speak any words. I sat blank-minded in my cell, the mess halls, and was quietly reserved during chore times. I was scared of what was happening inside of me and didn't know what to do to release the story that burned within. I had to tell it, even if it took years or decades to get it out. One day, I picked up a pen and paper and wrote freely about whatever came into my mind.

I hate cigarette smoke. The fumes get me hotter than the flame that births the poison. I hope I don't offend any of you that do smoke, but I have my reasons why I do not possess a tolerance for it.

Maybe it's just the fact that right now I'm sitting in a room filled with the air polluting white stuff. Or maybe it's because the strange bitch next to me, who just dropped some sexual innuendos in my ear, is puffing away. Or maybe, it's just because I'm in this damn place right now.

A year ago, I would have never dreamed that I would be sitting here at this moment. It's amazing how the entire course of your life can change just from meeting one person...

BIOGRAPHY

Kelly O'Callan lives in a suburb of Philadelphia, Pennsylvania, with her husband, two sons, and a dog named Jake. She enjoys writing fiction in a variety of genres, with psychological thrillers being her favorite. Her current published works include: *Breaking Limbo*, *Another Birthday*, *Operation Adam and Eve*, *Humility*, and *I'm Too Sexy*. She has plans to release a novel, titled, *Other People*, in Spring 2014.

Ms. O'Callan can be contacted at <u>kellyocallan@aol.com</u>, and found on Facebook, Twitter, and Goodreads.

Her blogs can be found on Goodreads and at www.kellyocallan.wordpress.com

24633314R00118

Made in the USA
Charleston, SC
30 November 2013